But Is He Jewish?
and Other Quirky Tales

Daniel Wolf

Contents

MISHEGAS

ANIMALS WITH ATTITUDES

QUIRKY TALES

Escape from Alcatraz

Bernard Levin and Milton Abramson are the only two men to have succeeded in escaping from the notorious prison-fortress of Alcatraz. They bade farewell as they reached shore upon their small floating device, yet Bernard could see Milton was unhappy about something. Years later, they chanced to meet, and Bernard asked Milton what was troubling him that night so long ago. Without missing a beat, Milton replied that he had wanted to row.

THE WALL

Saul Friedman had always wanted to visit the Wailing Wall in Jerusalem. Finally, retirement enabled him to fly to Israel. Unfortunately, Saul's eyesight had deteriorated in the course of his long career as a tailor. As a result, he could not read the directions to the Wailing Wall. Further, he was a prideful man and could not bring himself to seek help. Thus, he left Israel without achieving the object of his trip. Upon his return, his friend Nate initiated the following exchange:

Nate:	So tell me about the wall.

Saul:	It wasn't there.

Nate:	What do you mean "wasn't there"?

Saul:	It wasn't there.

Nate:	How could it not be there? It's a two-thousand-year-old wall. It doesn't just walk away.

Saul:	I tell you, I looked, and it wasn't there.

Nate:	Then where was it?

Saul:	It's on tour.

Nate:	What do you mean "on tour"?

Saul:	That's what they said. It's on tour.

Nate: So, where is it?

Saul: China.

Nate: China? They already have a wall. What do they need with our wall?

Saul: How should I know? What, I'm suddenly an expert in foreign affairs?

Nate: I'm just asking.

Saul: Enough already. What about you?

Nate: Rose and I are planning a trip to Niagara Falls.

Saul: You sure? Better check.

Nate: Why?

Saul: Might be on tour.

TIME MACHINE

Doctor Allen Katz, having invented a time machine, entertained the notion of revisiting his childhood. "Ah," he thought, "to feel the warm embrace of my mother again; to receive wise counsel from my father; to sit on the lap of my grandfather, listening to stories of Jews of olden days in Russia; and to savor the culinary masterpieces of my beloved grandmother: these experiences I am so looking forward to." Allen then recalled his other relatives, such as Uncle Al, who bought him his first bicycle; Uncle Leonard, who encouraged him to read the classics; and Aunt Goldie, who knew more about baseball than most sportswriters. Them, too, he wanted to see. Not least of all, he pictured his two best friends, Joe and Irv, and the good times they shared playing football, throwing snowballs, or simply watching their favorite TV shows. He could hardly wait to join them again.

After careful preparation, it was time to pull the lever, but at the last moment Allen stayed his hand—for no way was he going to repeat Miss Roman's third-grade class. No way!

A Short Story

When Paramount Pictures announced the signing of Jeff Goldblum, an elegantly imposing actor over six feet tall, to play Gerhardt Fibling, the iconic Jewish dwarf,[1] shock waves stunned his audience and rippled through the entire film industry. How could a man of his stature take on such a role?

Not only was the public thunderstruck, but Jeff Goldblum himself had aired his misgivings about the suitability of the match so audibly that negotiations had nearly been scuttled. The studio assured him that through special effects, they could make him appear dwarfish. However, this did not satisfy Mr. Goldblum, who, as a method actor, aspired not merely to enact but rather to *become* Gerhardt Fibling. Accordingly, Goldblum had sections of his legs removed to reduce his height.

Though Paramount professed to admire Mr. Goldblum's level of commitment in its press release, in reality, the casting department regarded him as deranged and soon had his contract declared null and void. The role was then offered to another highly esteemed Jewish actor, who was not as tall as Jeff Goldblum. Still, he too had been trained in the Method and had sections of his legs removed. As a result, he, likewise, was dismissed.

And so, the torch was passed from one Jewish actor to another. All, as it happened, were tallish; all adhered to the Method; all, upon accepting the role, chose to have sections of their legs removed; and each suffered

---

1. **A Meandering Note**
   Gerhardt Fibling's claim to fame is that using his knowledge of chemical engineering, he expanded the diameter of certain pipes in the plumbing at Auschwitz, thus enabling his fellow dwarfs to climb through to freedom. All made it out safely except one Johannes Fiddler, whom the Nazis killed as he reached the crematorium's roof. This story has led to speculation that the musical *Fiddler on the Roof* is not based on the Sholem Aleichem stories but instead inspired by the tragic and untimely end of Johannes Fiddler.

the same consequences. Finally, the studio executives returned from lunch and, detecting an unhealthy pattern, sensibly offered the role to Dustin Hoffman, for he was diminutive not only physically but also in box office appeal, thus saving Paramount considerable expense in salary.

What, then, was to be done with the lead actors whose bodies and careers had been wrecked? After careful deliberation, the big brains in the studio decided they should return as extras, thus replacing the natural dwarfs who had initially signed. Here, too, the consequences were grave, as the dwarfs mobilized to file a class-action lawsuit claiming breach of contract. This led the director to quip that "class-action" was an appropriate term since the assembled dwarfs looked "eerily similar to a first-grade class." This careless remark resulted not only in five nights of rioting with hundreds of casualties but also in the creation of an organization known today as Short Lives Matter.

THE TAIL

Despite some differences in perception and outlook that might be attributed to their respective religious backgrounds, Abe Fishman and Tom Finley had been close companions from boyhood onward and not merely as classmates in grade school. Though their lives had taken diverging paths in adulthood, Abe (a high-end financial adviser) and Tom (a construction worker) enjoyed an enduring friendship. Often they would meet for a drink and talk freely about unsurprising topics, such as sports, family, and work, until one day the conversation took a strange and fateful turn.

Tom: Abe, listen. I know what I'm about to say may be embarrassing, but there's this guy on my construction crew who . . . oh, forget it. Never mind.

Abe: Go ahead. What is it?

Tom: Please don't be offended.

Abe: You know me. It takes a lot to get me offended.

Tom: Well—and again, this is from him, not from me.

Abe: Certainly. I understand.

Tom: He claims—all right, here goes—he claims Jews have tails.

Abe: *What?*

Tom: That's what he said: "Jews have tails." Of course, I told him that's preposterous, but he's wholly convinced of it.

Abe: Well, you should have rapped him one. Such a thing. "Jews have tails." Lucky for him I wasn't there. I would have laid him flat.

Tom: You're right. Anyway, that's what he said.

Abe: Well, I hope you set him straight.

Tom: Well . . . kinda.

Abe: What do you mean, "kinda"?

Tom: Abe, to be honest, I'm a little curious. *Do* Jews have tails?

Abe: I can't believe what you just said. We grew up together. You know I don't have a tail.

Tom: Yeah, I know, but I must admit I never thought of looking. I mean, we took showers at the swim club, but somehow I never intentionally looked.

Abe: What are you saying—you wanna *check*?

Tom: If it's not too much trouble. My idea is, we go in the men's room; you drop your pants, turn around, and let me see.

Abe: Are you out of your mind? How can you ask such a thing? I should go to the men's room and show I don't have a tail? I can't believe we're even talking like this.

Tom: It'll take a minute. If you don't have a tail, I swear tomorrow, when I see him, I'll rap him right in the kisser.

Abe: Forget it. I'm not doing it.

Tom: Please?

Abe: Are you insane? Now stop it, or I'm gonna walk right out of here, and you'll never see me again. *I* swear.

Tom: What's so hard?

Abe: I'm serious, Tom. One more word and I'm leaving.

Tom: What am I asking? A minute, not even that.

Abe: Did you hear me? Such a thing. I should go to the men's room because you think I have a tail. Where you from—the Middle Ages?

Tom: One look.

Abe: That's it—we're done. Don't ever call. And if you happen to see me, act like you don't know me.

Abe rushed off in extreme distress, leaving his friend hunched over a mug of beer. He remained agitated not because of Tom's inappropriate, possibly voyeuristic curiosity, nor because Tom would not accept his word, but because he did, in fact, have a tail! Abe was one of those rare infants born with a tail, owing to a developmental disorder within the womb—the failure of a normally temporary embryonic structure to disappear early in pregnancy. Thus, he was faced with an ethical dilemma: Should he have acceded to Tom's request and exposed his tail, explaining it was a particular congenital abnormality and not a trait of all Jewish people? Or was it correct to express outrage, thus saving himself and world Jewry from certain moral opprobrium?

Abe pondered this grave matter for weeks. Then, at last, when the conflict had overwhelmed him, he succumbed to despair and committed suicide, leaving a cryptic note: "I have a tale."

At the funeral, friends and family debated in whispers the meaning of the note. What tale did Abe want to tell? What backstory had escaped their notice? As the rabbi conducted the service, discoursing gently about the unfathomable, the unknowable motives in each human soul, he knew not that the man sitting alone in the shadowy rear of the sanctuary was Tom—the one person who did indeed know what the note signified.

During their intimate years in grade school, Tom had been aware of Abe's receiving consistently low scores on spelling tests. Thus he was sure Abe meant to spell t-a-i-l, not t-a-l-e. Now enlightened and thus armed, Tom Finley soon launched one of the most virulent anti-Semitic campaigns in recent history.

THE EXOTIC SHOWER GIRL

Sheila Nussbaum came from a hardworking, lower-middle-class Jewish family. Though not exceptionally bright, she managed to earn a bachelor's degree from Temple University in Philadelphia in 1973. But times were hard for graduates, and Sheila toiled hour after hour sending out resumes and attending interviews, to no avail. However, she possessed one outstanding advantage—she was beautiful, and not subtly so. Aware of Sheila's frustration but even more aware of her dazzling appeal, an enterprising friend suggested she seek a position at a strip joint or what is commonly referred to as a gentleman's club.

Sheila was shocked at the very thought of it. After all, she had been raised in a proper Jewish home, one that observed Sabbath, kept kosher, and displayed a deep concern for the suffering of others. But, unfortunately, though her parents helped financially as much as possible, Sheila's funds were rapidly dissipating. And so, counter to what might be expected of a person with such high moral fiber, she applied for work at Garden Delight Gentleman's Club.

Mike Shane, the proprietor, took an immediate liking to Sheila—and not because they were coreligionists. Nevertheless, he maintained a professional demeanor, explaining that he had enough strippers but needed a good-looking woman to wear a string bikini and take a shower while men gazed and gawked. She would perform five days a week: Tuesday to Saturday from 8:00 p.m. to midnight. Of course, the club would provide soap, shampoo, and towels. Repelled at first, Sheila felt she had no choice. Funds were drying up, and it pained her to ask her parents for money each week. Thus, in a dramatic departure from the proprieties Sheila had learned at home and Hebrew school, she agreed to become Garden Delight's Exotic Shower Girl.

The first few weeks were nightmarish. Sheila was turned off by the musky scents of the club's brand of soap and shampoo—they were too provocative for her sensibility—and the towels were abrasive against her delicate skin. But once she had settled into the routine, she was permitted to use her own toiletries at the club's expense, so long as she furnished the receipts. She viewed this minor concession as a harbinger of significant victories to come—which it was, up to a point.

Sheila became a sensation, attracting men from all over the tristate area. Moreover, after each performance, she was, so to speak, showered with solicitous tips such as "Be careful not to slip on the soap" and "Don't use so much shampoo. It's concentrated." Though grateful for the verbal tips, she would have preferred the monetary kind—but she was too humble to ask. "Proper Jewish girls should not be too outspoken," she remembered her parents saying.

After a few months, it occurred to Sheila that she had not taken a shower in her apartment since starting the job. "What a fool I have been!" she thought. "Why send the Philadelphia Water Department money when I can shower at work?" As her parents had taught her to be frugal, she contacted the department and cut service. Thus, the salary she received combined with the money she saved by cutting service set Sheila on the path to financial independence.

One should like to foretell that Sheila, skillfully deploying her newfound wealth, would eventually become one of the most renowned women in the world. She would be the subject of books, movies, television specials, and even a Broadway musical called *Towels*. She'd wallow in the company of presidents, royalty, and media tycoons; her face would adorn glossy magazine covers; and her poster would be hung in the bedroom of every young girl whose dream was to be an exotic shower girl like their heroine, Sheila Nussbaum.

But no: it was not to be. As she aged, Sheila's appearance became problematic. With time, she transitioned from a string bikini to a less skimpy bikini to a modest one-piece tank suit. The daily shampooing had so damaged her hair she now wore a shower cap, and she had slipped so many times on the soap that she now wore giant flippers. Finally, since the soap irritated her eyes, she protected them with a snorkeling mask. In short, all she needed was a harpoon to be outfitted for deep-sea diving. Also, since Sheila had become frumpy, men were no longer interested. After all, if they wanted to see a dowdy woman take a shower, they could stay home, watch their wives, and avoid a cover charge plus a two-drink minimum.

Thus ends the saga of Sheila Nussbaum, the almost-idol—but a simple coda is in order. She was denied Social Security since the government had no listing for the profession of Exotic Shower Girl. The intervention of her congressman was required to secure the benefits she so desperately needed. Now old and alone in a bleak efficiency apartment, Sheila had only one remaining task—call the Philadelphia Water Department and restore service.

The Animal Lover

Barry Sussman loved interactive animal shows. Whenever he attended a performance, he offered to take part. For instance, he played volleyball with dolphins, danced with a bear, and was pickpocketed by a monkey. So it was at an elephant show at Safari World in Bangkok, Thailand, that he volunteered to lie on the ground as an elephant held one leg slightly over his head. However, unbeknownst to Barry and the elephant trainer, the elephant had just learned that his best friend had slept with his wife and—injury upon outrage—was demanding a ton of bamboo shoots as tribute, or else he'd trumpet his exploits to the entire herd. Thus dazed, confused, and angry at the blackmail, the elephant stepped on Barry's head.

This caused Barry no small degree of embarrassment. Hats no longer fit, nor could he part his hair in the middle, as he had no middle. The only consolation was that a flattened head enabled him to see through cracks. Even this skill was no grand prize for a man who was by nature not a voyeur. But the most devastating damage was that Barry's faith in animals was lost—crushed really—which led him to seek counseling.

The psychotherapist suggested that Barry participate without delay in another animal show so the mistrust would not linger. Thus, Barry boarded a plane back to Thailand and went directly to the world-famous Sriracha Tiger Show, where he volunteered to place his head in a tiger's mouth. However, unbeknownst to Barry and the tiger trainer, the tiger had just learned that his best friend had slept with his wife and—injury upon outrage—was demanding a ton of ground beef as tribute, or else he'd roar his exploits to the entire streak. Thus dazed, confused, and angry at the blackmail, the tiger snapped off Barry's head.

Are there any lessons to be learned from this distressing story? Yes, two. One, enjoy the sights and sounds of Thailand but never volunteer at either Safari World or the Sriracha Tiger Show. And two, quit while you're ahead or, more precisely, while you still have a head.

L'Affaire A-hole

Sy Blyweiss was pickpocketed at a nudist colony and immediately reported the theft to the police. Through a combination of state-of-the-art proctology and forensic science, investigators gathered and identified the culprit's fingerprints.

Unfortunately, the required procedure was so invasive and administered so frequently that Sy began to have second thoughts about the whole (hole?) thing. Nevertheless, he chose to endure the torment since he was raised in a family that believed fervently in the words of the Mishnaic rabbi, Simeon ben Gamliel, who declared, "The world rests on three things: justice, truth, and peace." Thus, hoping to save the world by restoring at least one of the three pillars (justice), Sy felt compelled to call the authorities in the first place.

To Sy's dismay, what began as a minor blip morphed into a daily feature on the local news and was soon covered by both the national and the international press. Regularly scheduled programming was interrupted for ***BREAKING NEWS!!!!*** concerning what the headlines dubbed "The A-hole Incident" in the United States or "L'Affaire A-hole" in France. The incident also became the butt of so many jokes on late-night television that Sy hid under his bed for nearly a week. His only rock of support was his wife, Leona, who meant to boost his morale by pointing out soothingly, "At least the thief knew where you were hiding the money. Otherwise, he would have ransacked the house."

Months later, after the perpetrator had been caught and confessed, the media frenzy subsided. Nevertheless, there were consequences. The mayor took credit for the capture and, as a result, was elected governor. The then incumbent governor also claimed credit and is now president of the United States. Sy changed his name and enrolled in the Butt Master Workout program, hoping to lose twenty pounds and return to

society. Leona divorced Sy and now hosts an entertaining television show, *Asinine Afternoons with Leona*. The actual police investigators refused all enticements, preferring to remain professionally credible.

Finally, the proctologist advertised that he had played a significant role in the capture and conviction of the thief. As a result, his business boomed, allowing him to retire early, move to Cambodia, and indulge his passion for drink.

THE DITCH DIGGER

When Melvin Horvitz was about to graduate high school, his father placed hands on the young man's shoulders and solemnly delivered these words: "Son, I don't care what you do in life so long as you are outstanding. If you choose to be a ditch digger, for example, I want you to be the best ditch digger there ever was."

Melvin, who had always yearned for approval from his stern and austere father, eagerly took this advice and undertook to be the best ditch digger in all human history. Thus, after graduation, he promptly joined a construction crew and, through serious application, blossomed into an exceptional ditch digger.

As his renown increased, people from nearly all the world's one hundred ninety countries came to watch Melvin dig ditches. His autobiography, *From Rags to Ditches* (his father owned a garment factory), swiftly jumped to first place on the *New York Times* Bestseller list. Also, due to Melvin's lobbying effort, ditch-digging was registered as an Olympic sport.

However, a drawback to Melvin's prominence emerged: namely, that young boys and girls refused to wash their faces at night, insisting they should "be like Mel." The problem became so pervasive that Melvin agreed to appear on national television, explaining to children the importance of washing before "hitting the sack." The broadcast so inspired American conservatives that they launched a national campaign to replace sex education with face-washing.

As a result of this event, Melvin was not only a media sensation but also such a formidable civic influencer that local political operatives encouraged him to run for mayor under the slogan "The city's in a ditch.

Only Mel Horvitz can pull us out." But after much deliberation, Melvin announced that since ditch-digging was his true calling , he had decided not to seek public office.

Melvin remained a figure of national and even international stature. However, his pride was fatally wounded when he attempted to reconnect with his father after years without meaningful communication. Melvin's overtures were received with words of contempt: "You moron, I didn't mean for you to be a ditch digger. I was only using that as an example. I wanted you to be a doctor or a lawyer like your older brother, not a lousy ditch digger, dumb-ass!"

The confrontation left Melvin so distraught that he followed King Saul's example from nearly three thousand years ago and fell on his shovel. The irony is that Melvin took his life during the coldest week of the year. The ground was so hard that workers at Avodah Memorial Cemetery could not dig, yes, a ditch.

PS: Melvin had a younger brother Stanley, who, throughout adolescence, said inappropriate things to women. In response, women told him, "Your mind's in the gutter." As a result, Stanley became a plumber.

V

The World Was Created for Me

Though Steve Lipmann led a secular life in practical terms, he was fascinated by Jewish texts, especially the Talmud. It thus buoyed him to read, "The world was created for me" in Sanhedrin 37B. "Imagine that," he thought. "I, Steve Lipmann, who graduated in the bottom quintile of my high school class, who took my cousin to the prom because I couldn't attract a real date, and whose parents said they wouldn't pay the ransom were I kidnapped—still, the world was created for me."

This discovery brought a spring to Steve's step. It gave him confidence when courting ladies, conferring with management in the workplace, or refusing panhandlers. This vibrant feeling extended even to such mundane activities as laundering his garments, escorting his sister to the orthodontist, or outwitting his father at chess. "Wonder of wonders," he would giddily repeat to himself, "the world was created for me."

However, the euphoria was bound to end, and it did after Steve made an otherwise unremarkable trip to the supermarket. In the checkout line, he chanced to meet a shopper who introduced himself as Moe. The interaction was so pleasant that they agreed to a drink at a nearby tavern the following evening. After the second round of beer, their conversation became even more amiable—that is, until Moe leaned over and confided, "Listen, Steve, I gotta tell you something."

"Be my guest," Steve smiled.

Moe announced solemnly, "The world was created for me."

"What?" Steve spluttered in shock, nearly overturning his tankard.

"Yes, the world was created for me. It was created solely for my benefit, and I am the center of all things."

"That's impossible," Steve countered indignantly. "The world was not created for *you*. The world was created for *me*. Where the hell do you get off saying the world was created for you, huh? Where the *hell* do you get off?"

"Sorry to break the news to ya, kid," Moe responded smugly.

"I'm not your kid."

"Maybe we should take this in the back," Moe suggested with just a hint of menace.

"My pleasure," Steve growled.

The two stomped out the door to a spot behind the tavern, and amid the punching, kicking, head butts, and body-slamming, heated words were exchanged.

"The world was created for me!" Steve roared.

"Was not. It was created for me!" Moe bellowed.

"Was not!"

"Was!"

The bartender called the police, and soon both men found themselves standing before a judge. "Now, what are you two punks fighting about?" the judge demanded sternly.

Steve spoke first. "This guy asserts the world was created for him, and I told him the world was created for me."

"Was not," retorted Moe.

"Was," insisted Steve.

The judge rendered a Solomonic solution. "I will divide the calendar year in half. You, Steve, will have January to June, during which time you can say the world was created for you. I'll give Moe July to December, during which time he can say the world was created for him. Either you take my offer, or it's ten days in the slammer for each of ya. Got it?"

Both men felt compelled to accept the judge's ruling, though Steve would have preferred July to December since he was more baseball than football. As it turned out, the situation changed dramatically within a few hours, when another pair of men appeared in court, each claiming the world was created for him. Applying the same principle, the judge now divided the calendar year into four segments.

The following day, Steve received a text message stating that he'd been reassigned July to September. Though he did not get the World Series, he was satisfied to get the heart of the baseball season. Still, in the belief that the World Series was created for him, Steve petitioned the judge to include October.

The Butcher of Treblinka

Twenty minutes before the bris was to begin, Moishe Kapinsky approached his nephew, Leonard, the infant's father. "Lenny, I'm looking and looking and thinking, where do I know this guy?"

"What guy?" asked Leonard with a puzzled frown.

"The mohel. I mean, I know I've seen him before, then it hits me. He's Friedrich Almer, the Butcher of Treblinka!"

"Friedrich Almer?"

"Yes."

"And he's *what?*"

"The Butcher of Treblinka."

Leonard rolled his eyes. "Of course, a hidden Nazi. Invading my house, yet."

"That's right."

"So let me get this straight. A notorious hidden Nazi is about to perform a circumcision on my son?"

"Yes, and you have to stop this right away. You cannot let that man get near the boy."

Leonard patted Moishe affectionately and summoned his patience. "Uncle Moish, I love you and respect you, and I know how your unspeakable suffering in the camps haunts you. But you're talking nonsense.

He's no hidden Nazi. His name's Alex Haberman, and he's a board-certified mohel. He comes highly recommended. I can assure you; Rabbi Abraham would not steer me wrong."

"What about the other mohel—Cutler, I think his name is?"

"He's in Israel. He won't be back till next week, so the rabbi suggested this man."

"So cancel till next week."

"Stop it. No one cancels a bris. You know the law—eight days after birth. Eight, not fifteen."

"Please—they'll understand."

"Who will understand? What, I should make an announcement? 'My dear family and friends, thank you for coming, but we must postpone till next week because my uncle Moish thinks the mohel is a hidden Nazi. Of course, you're welcome to take home whatever food you like. Just return the plates when you come back.'"

Growing increasingly passionate, Moishe entreated, "Listen, I remember. He has a tattoo of the Iron Cross on his right forearm. Ask him to take off his jacket. You'll see."

"Except he's wearing a suit, which means he's wearing a long-sleeved shirt. Or should I have him perform the bris in the nude?"

"Then I'll do it!"

Leonard grabbed his uncle's arm. "You'll do no such thing. Today's the most important day in my life and my wife's—the bris of our firstborn, and you'll do no such thing. Any more of this nonsense, and I'll ask you to leave. Now go to the bathroom if you need, 'cause we're starting in a few minutes." Stung and humiliated, Moishe retreated without another word.

The bris was executed as planned, flawless with no complications. Soon after, everyone moved into the dining room to feast on foods prepared by the local Jewish delicatessen. Everyone, that is, except Moishe, who sat silently in the living room clutching a drink. His sister, Ceil, soon pounced upon him.

"What's wrong with you?" she scolded. "Everyone's having a good time. Why you sitting alone? Come in. The food's out of this world. You've got to try the creamed herring. Bring me some the next time you come over."

"I'm not hungry," he growled.

"How can you not be hungry? You haven't eaten all day. Come in. It's not right. You have to celebrate."

"Give me a minute."

Moishe took a few deep breaths then entered the dining room and chose a seat at the far end of the table. He was careful not to make eye contact with the mohel, who was busy entertaining his rapt audience with what all agreed were hilarious jokes. Finally, the mohel announced that he had an appointment elsewhere and must depart. All stood respectfully in line as he made his way to the front door—all, that is, except Moishe, who remained seated. Ceil stood over him imposingly.

"The mohel's leaving. Say goodbye."

"He can leave without me."

"Moish, I'm so angry with you! Think no one sees? Everyone's whispering, 'What's wrong with your brother? Why is he acting this way?' Now stand up, be a mensch, and say goodbye. I want to go home."

Moishe left his seat and stood stiffly, stonily, next to Leonard, who was bidding an effusive farewell to the mohel. "We are so grateful," Leonard said warmly, gripping the mohel's hand.

The mohel flashed a perfunctory smile and carefully withdrew his hand. "Sorry, I have to go. I have another bris at two o'clock. You have a fine young man there. I can see it."

"I'll tell Rabbi Abraham how pleased we are."

The mohel nodded humbly. "I'd appreciate that. I can use the work."

Leonard reached out once more. "Before you go, may I introduce my uncle, Uncle Moish—Moishe Kapinsky." Then, after an awkward pause, he added solemnly, "He's a Holocaust survivor."

"Is that so? May I speak with him in private?" the mohel asked.

"Of course. Let me get back to my guests, and thanks again for your kind service." Leonard left the room, and Moishe was alone with the mohel.

"So good to see you again, Herr Kapinsky. You're looking vell. See you gained some veight, huh?"

Moishe recoiled from his tormentor's agreeable manner and easygoing appraisal. His voice was hoarse and choked with suppressed rage. "You bastard."

"Ah, now can't vee let bygones be bygones?" The mohel chuckled. "You know, you almost had me there. I'm vearing a short-sleeved shirt. Auf wiedersehen!"

The Meaning of Life

Even as a child, Ben Levy was notably curious. *How do flowers grow? Why is it that the earth revolves around the sun and not the sun around the earth? What causes earthquakes?*—these were among the many questions Ben asked his parents and teachers. However, as he got older and became more established, he sought the solution to only one—apparently overarching—problem: *What is life all about?* Thus, he talked with and observed people in everyday situations, hoping to discover the answer.

Perhaps life is about love, he thought. Ben needed to look no further than his own family, seeing how his parents continually quarreled and that his older brother had already been married and divorced twice. He therefore concluded that love was not what life was about. Perhaps, he ventured, the answer is wealth; but again, he had only to observe his uncle Seth, who was rich yet never seemed happy or content. He thus concluded that wealth was not what life was about.

Ben next pondered fame, but as a devotee of supermarket tabloids, he was well aware of movie and television stars who had died from a drug overdose. He thus judged that fame was not what life was about. And so he continued along this course. Ben's investigations led him to analyze such phenomena as craftsmanship, scholarship, athleticism, and even philanthropy, but in each case, despite his steady aim, he came short of the mark.

In time, Ben became despondent. He asked himself plaintively, "Am I to plod through life in ignorance of what life is all about?"

But out of nowhere, a miracle occurred. Ben received an invitation to attend his niece's bat mitzvah. Following the meal, the disc jockey assembled everyone in the middle of the dance floor. "Listen up," he announced. "We're going to do 'The Hokey Pokey'!" He started the music and sang:

> You put your left foot in
> You put your left foot out
> You put your left foot in
> And you shake it all about
> You do the hokey pokey
> And you turn yourself around
> That's what it's all about.

Ben was stunned. "Yes!" he shouted. "That's it! The Hokey Pokey! That's what life is all about. At last, my journey is over."

THE DENTIST

Nathan Birnbaum was once a one-man smiling machine. Wherever he went, he smiled because he had learned at an early age that smiles are contagious: that is, if you smile, someone will smile back. Not only did he smile, but he also sang "When You're Smiling" simultaneously. Moreover, if he passed someone on the street looking downcast, he'd say, "Smile—it's not so bad." Nathan was so committed to smiling that soon after receiving his bachelor's degree, he entered dental school to help people smile with more confidence.

It thus came as a shock when he discovered the excessive quantity of bacteria on seemingly healthy teeth. "What a fool I've been, encouraging people to smile," he muttered inwardly. "I should rather encourage them to keep their filthy mouths shut!"

Nathan thus became a one-man doom-and-gloom machine. Whether in the company of acquaintances, family, colleagues, or (of course) patients, he told distressing stories. He frightened everyone with reports of daily shootings, robberies, and vehicular accidents. He filled them with dread of natural disasters such as hurricanes, earthquakes, and floods. And even though he was aware of the more uplifting portions of Holy Scripture, he preferred to cite the plagues Moses visited upon the Egyptians—especially boils.

As a result, he never made friends, was rarely invited to parties, and was placed on the no-fly list as intelligence agencies considered him a threat to national morale. Though he was a skilled dentist, his practice suffered as he played funeral music in the waiting room. While treating a patient, he'd often sing "My Yiddishe Mama," considered one of the saddest songs ever written. His resonant bass boomed notably at these lines: "I long to hold her hands once more as in days gone by / And ask her to forgive me for things I did that made her cry." As for movies, he recommended such tearjerkers as *Marley & Me, Love*

Story, *Ghost*, and *Terms of Endearment*. But his favorite remained *Titanic,* especially from when the ship hit the iceberg.

Nathan never married, nor did he even make it past the first date. He was also banned by nearly every synagogue except during the Yizkor[2] service. In fact, he was once violently blocked from attending a Hanukkah celebration to the applause and cheers of the invited.

His brother agreed to deliver the eulogy at his funeral, which was attended by only a few who had either joined the service by mistake or been bribed for the sake of appearance. For nearly ten minutes, his brother stood silently. Then, finally, he summoned these words: "If you think it was bad knowing my brother, imagine *being* his brother," earning a standing ovation as he descended the pulpit.

____

2.   **Yizkor:** A memorial service for deceased relatives and martyrs.

THE ENGLISH LESSON

Murray Futterman had never particularly cared for Jewish women. He found them calculating, conniving, cunning, deceitful, discourteous, duplicitous, excitable, exhausting, impossible to satisfy, loud, malicious, mean-spirited, mercurial, overbearing, petty, rude, and spiteful. "And those are their good points," Murray would joke. Nevertheless, he was religiously observant and harbored hopes of marrying a Jewish woman and creating a proper Jewish home.

However, at thirty-five, he realized his prospects were dimming. Though he was content as a public school teacher, living in a modest inner-city one-bedroom apartment and driving a dated but reliable car, the women he pursued did not share his enthusiasm. Most were angling for someone of material substance—that is, a man with a vast investment portfolio, a house in one of the classier suburbs, and a car at least as desirable as a Lexus. So at this point, Murray contemplated a solution he had previously dismissed—marrying outside the faith. After all, he did not enjoy living alone and was haunted by the well-worn question, *Who's going to take care of you when you get old?*

At this time, it happened that a friend returned from touring Vietnam. Although the traveler described the region's features—the mountains, caves, and waterways—with great animation, what most caught Murray's attention was his friend's utterly approving impression of Vietnamese women, whom he found humble, appreciative, frugal, undemanding, and dutiful. "In short," his friend pointedly concluded, "the antithesis of an American Jewish woman."

So it came to pass that, during his summer vacation, Murray flew to Vietnam. After briefly acquainting himself with the natural and social environments, he set out on his quest. One afternoon, while strolling alongside a lake in the center of Hanoi's old quarter, he noticed a lovely young lady sitting on a bench.

Murray approached and gestured for permission to join her, which she unhesitatingly granted. Though neither could speak more than a few basic words of the other's language, they were comfortable in each other's company. They attended the famous water puppet show together that evening and saw each other whenever she was free from work. Eventually, Murray met her parents, gained their consent for the relationship, and started immigration procedures.

After six months, Ms. Le Hanh Binh, twenty-five years old, arrived at Philadelphia International Airport. The following day Murray introduced her to his mother, who, though cordial, was not enthusiastic about the prospect of a non-Jewish daughter-in-law. Still, she wanted her son to be happy, so she tried to be pleasant even though her disappointment could not be completely hidden. Later, he introduced her to his brother and various friends. Though all agreed she was stunning to behold and gracious in demeanor, they felt the language barrier presented an obstacle to mutual understanding.

By most measures, the arrangement was succeeding as Murray's friend had predicted. Binh was dutiful to a fault. She cooked sumptuous meals almost every evening, kept the apartment spotless, and even ironed his T-shirts. She also satisfied every conjugal need. "What more could I ask?" he congratulated himself. "She's perfect in every way. I have never been so joyful—never in my entire life." Thus, three months after her arrival, Murray and Binh married at City Hall and honeymooned at a Howard Johnson hotel in Atlantic City, New Jersey. "Why spend enormous sums on a honeymoon when she'll enjoy herself just as much staying at a Howard Johnson?" he reasoned.

Still, as predicted, the language barrier was taking its toll. Owing to poor communication, there were frequent misunderstandings, which sometimes erupted into anger on both sides. As a remedy, Murray enrolled her in a nearby language academy where she studied English conversation three hours each weekday. But after one month, he hadn't noticed any improvement in her speaking. It thus came as a shock when her teacher approached him with a delighted smile during the academy's year-end party.

"Your wife is making excellent progress," he said.

Murray was puzzled. "She is? I haven't heard a word of English."

"Believe me, in a few months, you'll think you married a native speaker."

"Are you sure we're talking about the same woman?" Murray asked.

"Le Hanh Binh from Vietnam?"

"That's right," Murray affirmed.

"I think she's waiting for the right moment. I'm sure you'll be pleasantly surprised."

A few weeks later, Murray received a phone call from the teacher. "Tonight's the night," the teacher announced. "She told me she's ready."

"Great!" Murray exclaimed. "I'll get a cake and some wine. I'll even set up my video cam to capture the big event. Thanks for all your help. I deeply appreciate what you've done for her."

Murray bought the most delectable-looking cake he could find, then hurried to a local winery for a bottle of its best vintage. He also searched a variety store for a family-size package of balloons and spent nearly an hour blowing them up. Finally, he set his video camera on a tripod to capture the historic moment when Binh would begin speaking.

At nine o'clock, Binh entered the apartment. He positioned her on the sofa, adjusted the lighting and camera, then sat next to her and delivered a preface to her speech:

"Good evening. I am here with my wife, Binh, who will speak at length in English for the first time in our marriage. It's a day I've been anticipating with both pride and suspense. And now may I introduce my wife, my lover, my best friend, and the person I value more than life itself—Ms. Le Hanh Binh." Murray rose from the sofa, readjusted the video camera, and gave her the signal to speak. Binh cleared her throat and began in a steady voice:

"Thank you for those words, Murray, and thanks for all the wonderful things you have done for me since I arrived in your country. I deeply appreciate it and will never forget your kindness. Still, there are several things I wish to say. First, I hate your mother. I never wish to speak to her again. If you have a family event, I'm not going. You go yourself. I hope never to lay eyes on that woman for the rest of my life. Next, what kind of man is a school teacher? Why couldn't you be a doctor or lawyer like your brother? Now that's a real professional, but a teacher? No way! Anyone can do that. My brother in Vietnam is a teacher, and he never even graduated high school. It's embarrassing telling people you're a teacher. Call yourself an educator, at least. That doesn't sound so bad. Also, how long are we going to live in this dump? Who

lives in an apartment? I'll tell you who lives in apartments—losers. Why can't we move to the suburbs like your brother and get a new car instead of that piece of crap you're driving? And maybe a maid, so I don't have to cook, clean, or do laundry anymore like I'm your servant, huh? And while we're on the subject of housework, how about some jewelry and new clothes for all my labor these past few months? Oh, yes, who goes to Atlantic City for a honeymoon and stays at a Howard Johnson's yet? I'll tell you who: l-o-s-e-r-s, losers. Finally, no sex tonight. I have a headache, and if you don't take me to the islands for a real vacation, I'm going to have this headache for a very long time."

Under normal circumstances, Murray would have been impressed by such linguistic competence and stylistic finesse, but somehow his mind was concentrated elsewhere.

CHANGES

Arnold had an abusive father. Nothing the child could say or do seemed to satisfy the parent. Even Arnold's manner of breathing was subjected to biting comment. "Who breathes like that?" his father admonished. "You breathe like *this*—watch me and listen." Though Arnold could not detect much difference between his father's breathing and his own, he chose not to argue, replying meekly, "I'll try to breathe like that from now on."

Eventually, the micromanaging of Arnold's every word and action resulted in a debilitating stutter, especially on words beginning with the *ch* sound. This was particularly burdensome for a sensitive boy living in Philadelphia, where the *ch*eesesteak is nearly as iconic as the Liberty Bell.

The stuttering had become especially acute by the middle of second grade. Thus, when he learned his third-grade teacher would be Ms. Chapman, Arnold was on the verge of panic, unable to enjoy the summer vacation. "How can I be in her class?" he fretted. "She'll think I'm rude if I can't say her name." As it turned out, Ms. Chapman was informed of Arnold's disorder before the fall term began and allowed him to call her "miss" throughout the school year. Similarly, each of his teachers from the fourth to sixth grades was alerted and made appropriate accommodations.

Middle school, however, did not provide this comfort. Students in that age group tend to be cruel and intolerant of even the slightest deviation. Particularly troubling was Arnold's English class, whose teacher, Ms. Harris, chose students at random to read aloud. One day, as they were reading a story called *Olympic Champions*, Arnold looked ahead. He noticed a paragraph that was a minefield of *ch* words such as *champion*, *cheer*, *challenge*, *chase*, and *Charles* Jacobus, who won a gold medal at the 1904 Olympic Games

in St. Louis. When they reached that spot, the teacher said, "Arnold, I haven't heard from you for a while. Please read the next paragraph."

"Ms. Harris, I'm not feeling well. May I please see the nurse?" Arnold requested.

"Of course. Just read the paragraph, then you can go," the teacher answered.

"But I don't feel well," Arnold pleaded.

"Arnold, it's a short paragraph. It will take you less than a minute, thirty seconds even. Then you may see the nurse."

Arnold stuttered on each of the *ch* words in the passage while his classmates laughed uproariously. News of this fiasco quickly spread throughout the building, and weeks passed before he was relieved from ridicule and mimicry in the hallways.

Arnold's only source of support was his mother. Though she tried to persuade her husband to be more sympathetic, she could advocate only so far, as she, too, was subject to his stinging rebukes. "You stay out of it," he commanded her. "Your job is to keep this house in order."

Arnold's father took a perverse delight in watching his son suffer, especially when ordering at a restaurant. "Do you feel like chicken tonight?" his father prompted.

"Sure," said Arnold.

"Well, I see today's specials are Chicken-in-the-Basket and Chicken Marsala. Which would you like?"

"I'll have the second one," Arnold said carefully, as he could not pronounce the word *chicken*.

"Which one was that?" his father pursued.

"Marsala," Arnold replied.

"Marsala? There's nothing here called Marsala," insisted his father, searching up and down the menu mockingly.

"Reuben, leave him alone," his mother interjected. "You know what he means."

"Of course I know what he means. I want to hear him say it."

"I can't! Okay, I can't. You know I can't," Arnold exploded as he banged his fist on the table.

"Arnold, it's all right. I'll order for you," his mother said consolingly.

Arnold's single pleasure was to play the guitar an uncle had given him for his bar mitzvah (fortunately, Hebrew does not contain the *ch* sound; thus, he could sing his Torah portion without much difficulty). In just a few years, Arnold had become a more-than-proficient musician. Not only had he taught himself to play, but he was able to execute some of the more iconic guitar licks by such artists as Jimmy Hendrix, the Rolling Stones, and the Beatles. In fact, he needed to hear a song only once before performing it, and with added embellishment.

Arnold's speech problems continued unabated in high school. Still, he found his classmates more accepting than the middle schoolers. He especially enjoyed the twice-weekly speech therapy sessions with Dr. Jefferson. Though his progress remained glacial, he was grateful for her warmth and refined understanding—qualities he rarely experienced at home. At one point, she invited Arnold's parents to a conference. She could immediately detect the locus of Arnold's difficulties as his father snorted, "I guess you want to talk about my idiot son. I'm sure we agree he can't do anything right."

Following high school, Arnold attended a two-year community college while still living at home. By this time, Arnold was making every effort to avoid speaking to or even seeing his father. Though his mother tried to repair the breach, it was insurmountable. Any chance for reconciliation had long since passed, as his father was either unwilling or unable to demonstrate any measure of empathy. He would grumble, for example, "I don't get what the problem is. Open your mouth and talk. What's so hard?"

Around this time, the rock musician David Bowie released a song called "Changes," during which he stutters on the title word. Though the song became wildly popular, cover bands performed it with only a modicum of success, as singers had difficulty producing the stutter. As it happened, a member of one rock band suddenly recalled Arnold from middle school. "I remember this kid who stuttered on *c-h* words," he told his colleagues. "I'll see if I can locate him, and maybe he can help us."

The search having succeeded, the two met at Arnold's home. Arnold agreed to help, then grabbed his guitar and performed the song flawlessly. Soon, Arnold was not only singing (stuttering) the word *changes* but he

had replaced the band's lead guitarist. In short order, the band became highly successful. In addition, for the first time, Arnold was making money, which led to the following exchange with his father:

Arnold: I'm moving out.

Father: With what?

Arnold: With my money—the money I'm making with the band.

Father: You think that's enough? There's more to moving out than just rent. There's food, heat, electricity. Bet you never thought of that. You don't have enough.

Arnold: I do. I will! And if I don't, my friends will help me.

Father: Friends? You have no friends. Your only friend is family.

Arnold: Family? You call this a family? You've been a thorn in my side from the day I was born. When were you ever a friend? All I've gotten from you is criticism. Why do you think I stutter? It's from you. You made me so nervous. You even criticized the way I breathe! Who criticizes that?

Father: I didn't like the way you were breathing.

Arnold: I was alive, wasn't I? Wasn't that enough? Do you have any idea what hell my life has been? I live in Philadelphia and can't order a ch-ch-ch cheesesteak. I go to McDonald's and can't order a ch-ch-ch cheeseburger. I can't make a friend whose first name begins with *C-h*. How can you have a friend if you can't say his name? You did this to me, so I'm moving out.

Father: You'll be back.

Arnold: Never!

Father: How you gonna pay tuition, big guy?

Arnold: You promised.

Father: Only if you live home.

Arnold: Then I'll drop out.

Father: Then be a dumb Jew like your uncle Al.

Arnold took an apartment with one of the band members. Though he called his mother every day and spoke to her at length, he only traded banal niceties with his father and only on occasion. In fact, the more he distanced himself from his father, the more his speech improved—gradually, yet distinctly. And, on account of his mother's insistence, his father resumed paying Arnold's tuition.

Eventually, Arnold left the band and became a successful studio musician who worked and sometimes toured with the day's reigning acts, including Britney Spears, Madonna, and Billy Joel. In his fifties, Arnold wrote a book about his career in the music industry and the famous entertainers he had gotten to know. After composing the first draft, he felt the book should serve some greater purpose and so drew from his experiences to add ten ways to overcome any obstacles life might present.

No doubt Arnold had his father in mind when he wrote Number 6: "Avoid negative people. Surround yourself with those who can support and encourage you." The book became a bestseller, especially among young people who not only enjoyed reading about celebrities but found his advice inspirational. Almost daily, Arnold received letters or e-mails saying how much the book had helped in their daily struggles.

Though Arnold lived in Los Angeles, he returned to Philadelphia every few months to see his parents. Through the years, he had developed several strategies to avoid or at least mitigate his stutter. Even so, his father, now in his eighties, was as critical as ever. When Arnold showed him a copy of his book, his father's only reaction was "Since when did you learn to write?" However, one day, when he was alone with his mother, she said, "Your father is very proud of you. Everywhere we go, he tells people what a success you've become."

"Then why did he make it so hard for me growing up?" Arnold asked.

"I don't know," his mother responded. "It wasn't easy for me either, if you recall."

Early one morning in Los Angeles, Arnold received word that his father had died in his sleep. He rushed to Philadelphia for the funeral and stayed past the shiva to help with financial matters. During the flight back, Arnold had time to reflect. Clearly, he and his father had never reconciled. Perhaps his father was simply

of a generation not given to emotion. Years later, he read a book arguing that opponents are necessary to help us grow spiritually. Perhaps, Arnold considered, his father's badgering had helped him develop as a human being. And yet, it was cold comfort, as he would have wished nothing more than to have had a warm, caring, and supportive father.

What Did He Mean?

In 1960, at the age of twenty-five, Sheldon Mermelstein entered a Philadelphia rabbinical college and soon became the center of attention. Whether discussing Torah, Midrash, or Talmud, he displayed near-clinical understanding, providing insights that aroused admiration and envy in classmates and faculty alike. In fact, he brought a store of knowledge so profound that many thought he already possessed the skills to be ordained.

Indeed, his associates would gladly have advanced Sheldon on the spot, without further instruction, to be relieved of his unpleasant presence. Though his intellect was of the first order, it was, by all accounts, overshadowed by his arrogance. Not a few times did he berate teachers with condescending offers, such as "Let me take over the class. Maybe you'll learn something" or sneers, such as "Did you earn your degree or buy it?" But arrogance is often a ruse designed to conceal unease. And so it was with Sheldon. He was homosexual and was not free.

Though he was handsome and many women found him appealing, he preferred the company of men. From Phillip Rosen in middle school to Fred Stein in high school to multiple affairs at Hebrew summer camp, Sheldon was simply more comfortable among men. Though he felt not a scintilla of guilt, it was still, in 1960, necessary to conceal his orientation since exposure could lead to expulsion from school and disgrace for his family.

Of course, Sheldon was all too aware of Judaism's attitude toward homosexuality: it was uncompromising in much of recorded doctrine. In particular, two passages from scripture—"You shall not lie with a male as with a woman" (Leviticus 18:22); and the even more severe "If a man cohabits with a male as with a woman, both have done an abominable thing; they shall be put to death" (Leviticus 20:13)—made it

imperative not to raise suspicion. Though he found sustenance in 2 Samuel with David saying of Jonathan, "Your love to me was more wonderful than the love of women" (1:26), he was sure this would carry little weight before an administrative committee.

Despite its liberal reputation, Philadelphia was at that time as repressive toward gays as any American city. Nevertheless, it accommodated a vibrant demimonde consisting of gay bars, bathhouses, and the infamous Merry-Go-Round. In this two-street area, gay men cruised or hopped into cars to service seemingly straight, suburban businessmen. Once introduced to this world, Sheldon flourished in defiance of his fears about discovery. Eventually, he moved out of the college dormitory and rented a modest efficiency a block from Rittenhouse Square, a famous Center City park and the locale for many of Sheldon's conquests.

He had a more or less standard modus operandi. He'd stroll through the park at night, seek out a seated middle-aged man, ask permission to join him, engage in some harmless banter, then propose going back to his place. Most accepted, though a few expressed outrage and quickly left. There was also the occasional reluctance, in which case he employed scripture for encouragement. He told the story of Queen Esther, who hesitated three days before entering King Ahasuerus's chamber. "As you can see," Sheldon would explain, "reluctance is normal. Even a queen can sometimes be hesitant."

Money was always an issue. Though he received a modest weekly stipend from his Brooklyn-based parents, it was inadequate, especially on weekends. Of course, there were many possible ways to replenish funds— he could wait tables at a kosher restaurant, teach Hebrew school on Sundays, or prepare students for their bar and bat mitzvahs. But in Sheldon's estimation, these were not adequate measures, as they would deprive him of valuable hours for cruising the Merry-Go-Round and Rittenhouse Square.

Soon enough, a solution emerged that addressed Sheldon's need for cash along with his desire to maintain a homosexual lifestyle—he could work as a prostitute. Whereas there was some theological flexibility regarding homosexuality, there was no such allowance for male prostitution. Still, the idea intrigued him. The advantage over a mainstream job was independence—he would control his schedule, fees, and working conditions. A further benefit was that this arrangement would provide more time for study.

At this time, Sheldon's father became seriously ill, and his parents could no longer afford to send the stipend, as their medical expenses had increased dramatically. "Perhaps, then, I *ought* to be a prostitute.

God might even see it as a good deed because I'm helping my parents hold on to their money," he advised himself—though he knew he was rationalizing.

Sheldon now cruised at night as before, but with the added business dimension. He decided to charge twenty-five dollars, which seemed to be the going rate. He was pleased with the result; there was no need to burden his family financially. Moreover, he had ample time to prepare for the upcoming final exams, which he anticipated respectfully. Indeed, there were indications that Sheldon would fulfill his religious role with sincere humility as he matured.

But one evening, a brief encounter put an end to tranquility. While making the usual tour around Rittenhouse Square, he sat down beside a man who, upon hearing the price, stood up, looked directly at Sheldon, and declared, "You're worth more than that" before leaving.

Sheldon gave this utterance no thought until the following morning, when suddenly it loomed large. The man's words—"You're worth more than that"—held him captive. "What did he mean? Did he mean I was too precious a soul to work as a prostitute, or did he mean I should charge thirty or even forty dollars? What did he mean?" The question bothered him so much that he returned to Rittenhouse that evening, sat on the same bench, and waited for the man to return. He did this every day for a month, to no avail.

Sheldon graduated, was ordained that spring, and found employment at a moderate-size synagogue just outside Philadelphia. There he performed his many duties faithfully. Still, whether he was leading High Holiday services, presiding over weddings and funerals, or preparing young people for their bar and bat mitzvahs, the question continued to nag—"What did he mean?" His duties often kept him busy at night, but on those rare free evenings, he drove to Rittenhouse Square and again sat on that same bench even though he had forgotten what the man looked like by now.

One day, as Sheldon was working in his office at the synagogue, the question overwhelmed him, and he shouted, "What did he mean? What did he mean?" so loudly that his secretary rushed in. "What did he mean, Carla? What did he mean?" Sheldon implored.

"Rabbi, I'm just a secretary. How can I know what He means? You, above all, should know of God's mysterious nature."

"I'm not talking about God," Sheldon answered.

"Then what *are* you talking about?"

"Uh . . ." he began, then retreated with "never mind," realizing he was skirting professional suicide.

Eventually, Sheldon married and raised a family, in large part for public consumption. At the same time, he discreetly acted on his secret sexual proclivity whenever possible. Though his wife always suspected, she said nothing, and only after her death did Sheldon reveal the truth to his children, who also had long suspected. As a professional, he was highly accomplished, becoming a best-selling author and a staple on television talk shows. He presided over White House prayer breakfasts, conducted the funeral service of an Israeli prime minister, and was granted a private audience with the pope. Yet for all his success, on occasion he found himself asking, "What did he mean?"

After decades the haunting question receded to the back of Sheldon's mind. Only when he was in the vicinity of Rittenhouse Square did it again force its way to his consciousness. Looking back, he wondered why he had become so obsessed with finding out. Was it God's way of punishing him for his behavior as a youth, or rather the result of some deep-seated guilt? He recalled that the man on the bench was in his mid to late forties; so now, some forty years later he might not even be alive. Or if by chance they happened to meet, he would most likely not remember the incident. "What did I mean? What did I mean about *what?*" the man would ask. And for Sheldon to provide context would be too embarrassing for both of them.

****

At the age of eighty-four, surrounded by family, friends, and colleagues, Sheldon lay dying. Though he tried to speak, his tyrannical sister, Helen, wouldn't let him. "Say no more, Sheldon. Your work is complete. You need to rest." But his four-year-old granddaughter, Rachel, made her way through the crowd and stood at the side of the bed.

"Grandpop, what do you want to say? Please tell us," she urged gently. All rebuked her: "Leave your grandfather alone! Let him rest."

Summoning his remaining strength, Sheldon propped himself up and spoke clearly with a strange, almost devilish smile. "When I was young, I studied to be a rabbi, and at night I worked as a prostitute." With that, he died.

For nearly a minute, all those gathered stood in stunned disbelief; then, a colleague broke the silence. "Let it be said that his last words were these: 'When I was young, I studied to be a rabbi, and at night I worked to unravel the mysteries of the Almighty.'"

All agreed, and soon word of his passing was disseminated to all major media outlets. "Today," CNN's Wolf Blitzer solemnly announced, "America and the world mourn the death of the distinguished rabbi Sheldon Mermelstein, whose reported last words were 'When I was young, I studied to be a rabbi, and at night I worked to unravel the mysteries of the Almighty.'"

As the soul left Sheldon's body, the angel Gabriel was there to guide him into the light. And as they came closer, Gabriel whispered into his ear, "He meant you should have charged thirty or even forty dollars." With that, Sheldon grinned as he had never done while living and, raising a fist, shouted, "Yes! Yes!"—for now he could truly rest in peace.

THE FABULOUS LIFE OF MARVIN LUTZ

arvin Lutz was a playboy. And why not? With his chiseled jaw, jet-black hair, and cleft chin, he was by all accounts the best approximation to a Jewish Cary Grant. Women of all ages found him irresistible. Indeed, he could claim to have lost track of how many had slipped him a phone number while he was sitting alone in a bar or restaurant, even if they were on a date. And women with whom he had ended a relationship would persistently camp outside his home until he had no recourse but to call the authorities. "If you don't see me, I'll kill myself!" they would scream as they were being restrained and hustled into the patrol car.

Besides being handsome, Marvin was a well-compensated corporate executive, drove an expensive sports car, wore tailor-made suits, and resided in a section of the city few could afford. He was a patron of the city's most celebrated restaurants, where he was continually spotted with yet another breathtakingly beautiful companion. Marvin was also on a first-name basis with many of the city's corporate and political elite and was frequently seen sitting next to the team owner at a sporting event.

His brother and two sisters married in their twenties or thirties, had children, and lived quiet, uneventful lives. "Dullsville" was Marvin's description of these arrangements, though his brother Jack, in particular, repeated the well-worn mantra, "Who's going to take care of you when you get old?" "I'll deal with that when the time comes," Marvin would counter. "It will come sooner than you think," Jack admonished.

Throughout his thirties, forties, and fifties, Marvin's life was notable for an endless series of female conquests. No relationship lasted more than a few months, and even then, he managed to juggle two or three flings on the side. Not only did women battle to be with him, but men also adopted his signature scowl, which seemed to say, "Tell me something I *don't* know."

At forty-five, he was profiled in the city's monthly magazine in a piece titled "The Fabulous Life of Marvin Lutz." He was quoted as stating, "I promise women nothing. I make it clear from the beginning that I have no interest in a long-term relationship or marriage. If a woman cannot accept that, hey, no hard feelings." The article concluded, "Marvin Lutz is the city's penultimate *bon vivant*. It's fair to say this is Marvin's world, and we're just lucky to be in it."

But by the time Marvin reached sixty, things had changed. Marvin was losing his looks. Either his nose had grown longer or his face had receded. His once abundant jet-black hair had thinned and turned grey, and his cleft chin was now competing with other chins. Women refused his advances or, if they agreed to go out, canceled at the last moment. Often Marvin sat home on a Saturday night, reduced to watching old movies on television.

Even some of his closest male buddies were abandoning him, preferring the company of younger, more dashing Lotharios. Worse were the times he'd venture into a bar or club, only to hear, "What's that old man doing here?" In fact, Marvin was becoming an object of ridicule, as he peppered his speech with terms such as *babe*, *chick*, and *broad*—a throwback to the 1950s and thus out of tune with the current politically correct environment.

At the age of seventy-five, Marvin, acknowledging his need for knee surgery, his failing eyesight, and his steadily multiplying chins ("My God, I look like a pelican!"), was living in solitude. His one remaining sister visited on occasion. "Well, Marvin," she lectured, "you have no one to blame but yourself. We warned you this day would come, but you refused to listen. How often did Jack tell you to settle down, get married, raise a family, be a mensch? I guess you thought the party would go on and on, right? Well, nothing lasts forever. I guess that's your problem—you never grew up."

With that, she left. Marvin sat for a moment, considered what his sister had said, then readily dismissed it. For even in his present state, he could look back and say with complete confidence that it had been a fabulous life.

My Aunt Died

My aunt died last year. She was my mother's sister. She died while her son was driving her home. She closed her eyes and passed away while sitting in the front seat. My mother still hasn't stopped talking about it:

Did you ever hear such a crazy thing—die in a car? Who dies in a car? You die on a bed in your home—not in a car. I tell you, her whole life, she couldn't do anything right. Not one thing. She married the wrong man, had a crazy son, and sold shmatas[3] in Kensington. Who sells shmatas in Kensington? You want to sell, you go to City Line, 69th Street—*that's* where you sell. And if you think you might die, you see a doctor, not pick up ice cream at Rite Aid. Who goes shopping when you feel you might die? I tell you who—my crazy sister, making life so hard for her son. Here he's driving her home, and that's when she decides to die? Let the man rest, for God's sake. He works hard all day and has to deal with this? Wait till you get home, like a normal person. Why even talk about it? She was never normal. On a Friday, yet! You die on a Monday or a Tuesday. *That's* when you die, not when everyone's made plans. And who dies in the summer? Maybe if you're royalty, fine. But my sister? Far from royalty. Once she won at bingo—her claim to fame. And her husband? No prize there. Who marries a man shorter than you? They looked like a comedy team, for God's sake. And her son, Bryan. Who names a Jewish boy "Bryan"—with a *y*, yet? What happened to "Sam" or "Harry"? "They're not modern names," she tells me. She knows modern? She served the same lousy meatloaf her entire life, and suddenly she's a maven of modern? And what kind of shiva was that—no whitefish, only cold cuts. Did you see herring? I didn't. And how do you eat a bagel without cutting it first? I'm ninety-three years old, and I'm soon gonna cut a bagel with a plastic knife? Then I ask,

---

3.   **Shmatas:** Rags, cheap goods.

"Where's the cream cheese?" "Oh, we don't serve cream cheese. We serve cream cheese *spread*," her husband tells me. I tell you, the whole family's nuts.

My Eulogy

Since I doubted anyone would take the time, I decided to write my eulogy. I begin by making some apologies; first, to the trees: I'm sorry I wasted the oxygen you provided me when it could have been put to better use, like low-flying party balloons. Next, to my parents: I'm sorry for the money you spent on me, such as braces for my teeth. Maybe looking like a rabbit would have gotten me further in life. Who knows? I could have been a lobbyist for the carrot industry.

I also wish to apologize to my teachers. I'm sorry you had to waste paper on me, and for the time it took to mark my tests, though receiving it back full of blood, sweat, and tears was not very professional, in my opinion. I also wish to apologize to anyone who passed me on the street. I'm sorry my lack of transparency blocked your view. Otherwise, you could have seen more aesthetic things such as billboards or fender bending accidents.

I know it's customary to relate some interesting things about the deceased. Still, looking back (as if I could look forward), my life was pretty much a consistent color of grey with occasional flourishes of neutral, faded, washed-out, and pale. Occasionally, I tried to make myself stand out by peppering conversations with stimulating quotes. But this rarely worked out, like the time I said, "As the saying goes, *A room without books is like a a body without a soul,*" to which my interlocutor replied (within earshot of hundreds), "Excuse me, but when quoting it's only appropriate to give full attribution. What you should have said was 'As the Roman philosopher and writer Marcus Tullius Cicero said, *A room without books is like a body without a soul.*' You could also have added that he lived from 106 to 43 BC."

Of course, as you know, my life consisted of a series of dead-end jobs such as cashier at Blockbuster, telephone switchboard operator, and milkman. My father, ever the jokester, suggested (again, within earshot of hundreds) I apply for Town Crier, although, in his defense, he did offer to buy the bell.

Also, as you know, I never found love except when playing tennis and the score was 15-love. As a result, I didn't have children. As they say (don't ask "As who says?" since I'm in no position to answer), "It's easy to make a baby but hard to support one." Unfortunately, in my case, it was the opposite.

Still, many told me to be thankful for the little things in life, which indeed I was. In fact, that's all I ever did—show thanks for little things. But where were the big things, huh? Where the hell were the big things? I certainly never experienced them. However, I did have some fond memories, especially of high school. It was the first time I had sex. Unfortunately, it was the last time I had sex.

Yes, many predicted I wouldn't go far, and they were right. I can't say it was a bumpy ride since most rides downhill are smooth with few obstacles. Now I'll rot under the earth, but I'm sure I'll find some way to screw this up too. In any event, I am grateful for *this* little thing—your courteous if brief, temporary, and fleeting attention. Goodbye.

ALAN FEIN

Throughout his life, Alan Fein experienced continual bad luck. Nothing worked out well, even when he performed a mitzvah.[4] For example, after saving a woman from drowning, he was arrested for groping. When he wrote a letter overflowing with heartfelt admiration to his favorite author, it was returned, red-penciled with corrections and comments such as "REDUNDANCY." In addition, he was burdened with a long, horse-like face, so wherever he went, people gave him carrots.

As a romantic young man, Alan spent a year building homes for the poor in India. To Alan's chagrin, one day a former US president briefly stopped at his village, banged a single nail into a wall, and won the Nobel Peace Prize. Then on the trip home from India, a United Airlines flight attendant accidentally spilled hot coffee onto Alan's lap. He tried to make light of it by joking, "Looks like the friendly skies of United are not so friendly today!"—but no one laughed.

Once resettled in the United States, Alan was determined to understand and appreciate cultures different from his own. Accordingly, he arranged to have lunch with a young black man, seeking to learn about hip-hop music. Much to Alan's disappointment, the young man revealed his favorite singers were Perry Como, Andy Williams, and Vic Damone. Another time, Alan had lunch with a Chinese man who, upon receiving the bill, asked Alan to check the math.

Desperate to find joy or at least laughter, Alan attempted to join a traveling circus. However, the clowns had aged and decided not to travel anymore. In search of spiritual guidance, Alan trekked for three weeks through the Himalayas, hoping to speak with The Wise Man of the Mountain. As the gracious sage was about to explain the meaning of life, he was stricken with acute laryngitis and rendered speechless.

---

4.   **Mitzvah:** A good deed.

Returning home exhausted, Alan discovered that his ex-wife had become a notorious porn star and performed for the public in ways she wouldn't with him. His then girlfriend decided to break up with him at a major league sporting event. Alan was shocked, horrified, and burst into tears. Unfortunately, the giant jumbotron captured the entire scene, as millions of fans watched (the game was nationally televised).

He had a younger brother with a checkered work history who happened to marry Miss Universe. When Alan reminded him of his checkered work history, his brother retorted, "Who cares about my checkered work history? I married Miss Universe!" This remark did not buoy Alan's spirits, to say the least. When he was about to turn fifty, he confided to a friend how much he enjoyed marching bands. In response, the friend hired a marching band to follow Alan for an entire day, which resulted in his dismissal as a hospital orderly in a maternity ward.

At the age of sixty-five, Alan was diagnosed with a terminal disease. The doctor told him he had one month to live. "What, thirty days?" Alan stammered in disbelief. "No," the doctor replied, "it's February."

With limited time remaining, Alan decided to take a sentimental journey. He returned to the hotel where he had lost his virginity decades ago, only to find that the site now housed the American Comedy Museum, and his room was labeled the centerpiece attraction. As he lay dying, no one came to visit. You see, in his final years, Alan found work as a florist. As a result, no one knew what to bring him.

Drinking Buddies

R on Drezner led a full and fortunate life. He had traveled extensively in the United States and abroad, spent half a year laboring on a kibbutz in Israel, and even climbed mountains in Nepal. Moreover, he had been happily married for nearly thirty years to his childhood sweetheart and ran a prosperous real estate company. In addition, he and his wife had raised two sons who were successful and now had beautiful families of their own. In short, Ron felt gratified both spiritually and materially.

And yet, there was one thing Ron regretted: he had never, even in college, drank at a bar with a group of men. He had only himself to blame. To begin with, he never liked the taste of beer. Further, he had a herniated spinal disc that caused discomfort when he sat for any length of time. But the main reason was that Ron was shy—he simply had trouble chatting with strangers.

Summoning courage, Ron determined to visit a neighborhood tavern, find a bunch of guys seated together, and ask to join. In preparation, he studied the sports pages, watched recently released movies, devoured popular television shows, and even read tabloids should the conversation veer in that direction. Thus fortified, Ron put on jeans, a comfortable sports shirt, and running shoes before setting out for Bernie's Tavern, just a few miles from home. Once inside, he surveyed the place and spotted a group of men toward the back. He ordered a beer, took a deep breath, and approached the table.

"Hi, guys, mind if I join?" Ron asked.

"Sure," one guy answered. "George, move down a little. Make some room for . . . what's your name?"

"Ron."

"Make space for Ron." A few guys moved down, and Ron was able to push in a chair.

"Let me introduce you," the same guy said. "That's George. This here's Tom, that's Phil, Ted, Pete, and I'm Ralph."

"Nice to meet you," Ron responded happily. So far, so good.

"What kind of business you in?" asked Pete, appraising him with narrowed eyes.

"Real estate," Ron answered.

"Real estate? Oh, God!" Tom groaned. "My sister just got fleeced by some Jew developer. Some kike named Steinberg."

"Hey, don't be surprised. Where there's money, there's always a Jew," Ted sagely supplied.

"Damn Jews. You can't see a movie without some Jew star or directed by that Christ-killer, Steven Spielberger," Ralph spluttered indignantly.

Ron had the impulse to correct Ralph but thought better of it. Instead, he tried to change the subject. "Phil, I see you have *Vietnam Vet* on your shirt. Did you serve?"

"Two tours. We would have won if it weren't for all the Jew commie traitors in the State Department," he asserted in disgust.

So it went all evening—the Jews this, the Jews that. They agreed to meet the following Wednesday, but Ron was noncommittal. Damn if he was going to reveal he had a synagogue men's club meeting scheduled that night.

POPULARITY

J ake Gittelman hated his younger brother Jerry so intensely that he stopped just short of wishing him dead. Not because Jerry had a checkered work history, bouncing from one job to the next, or because he and his family survived on the generosity of his father-in-law—though these facts were damning enough.
No, Jake simply could not tolerate that Jerry had so many friends.

Jake had never encountered anyone as popular or familiar as his brother. No matter where he was—on the street, at a sporting event, at a restaurant—everyone seemed to recognize Jerry. When he turned sixty, for instance, a surprise party was attended by over two hundred people. Yet previously, when Jake reached sixty, no one noticed—not even his wife.

Jake was particularly infuriated at B'nai B'rith lodge meetings, where men wrestled for the honor of removing Jerry's coat. Though he was not on the executive board, Jerry was given a seat next to the president and was consulted before any decision. All the while, Jake sat huddled in the back, sulking.

"How is it that a man who never graduated from college, can't hold a job, and needs his father-in-law to stay afloat could have so many friends?" Jake grumbled to his wife.

"Must be something about his personality," his wife hinted. "He's a pleasure to be around."

"And I'm not?" he challenged.

"Eat your soup, dear," his wife replied diplomatically.

****

In late December 2008, misfortune befell Jake. The Bernard Madoff scheme was uncovered, and he lost a great deal of money. Jerry called.

"I'm watching the news about Madoff. You had investments with him, right?" Jerry asked.

"That's right," Jake acknowledged curtly.

"Did you lose?"

"A lot."

"How much?"

"Around a million," Jake admitted.

"Don't worry. I'll help you out."

Jake was incredulous. "How you gonna do that?"

"You'll see."

Jerry contacted his legions of friends to describe his brother's predicament. Within a few weeks, Jake was made whole.

"I can't thank you enough," Jake said in a show of graciousness.

"Hey, what are brothers for? I'm sure you'd do the same for me."

"Of course," replied Jake—though he was sure he wouldn't.

Ambassador to the World

Though not ritually observant, Lee Aaronson was absorbed by reading ancient Jewish texts, particularly *Pirkei Avot* (*Chapters of the Fathers*; also known as *Wisdom of the Fathers* or *Ethics of the Fathers*). This is a tractate in the Mishna, composed between 190 and 230 CE, on moral-ethical life. He was especially taken by the probing words of Rabbi Hillel, who inquired, "If I'm not for myself, who shall be for me? But If I'm only for myself, what am I?" And "If not now, when?" (*Pirkei Avot* 1:14). However, one of Hillel's sayings—"Do not separate thyself from the community" (*Pirkei Avot* 2:4)—troubled Lee, since he could not abide the sight of another human being.

Though he tried for years to follow Hillel's dictum by joining clubs, becoming active in the synagogue, and participating in group excursions, he could not shake his profound dislike for people. As a result, he reverted to an even greater determination to avoid contact. He ordered in, took long walks at three o'clock in the morning, and never answered the phone—except, of course, calls from his long-suffering mother, who found her son, in a word, weird. "It's not good to be alone so much. You need to be with people, especially as a Jew. A Jew needs other people. It's how we've survived all these centuries."

He knew she was right. Rabbi Hillel had stated as much, claiming that society, not the private individual, is the more significant entity, as the community has more existence (*Derech Chaim* 2:40–44). Additional reading led him to Rabbi Avraham Kook, whose opinion was even harsher: "One who considers severing himself from the people must sever his soul from the source of its vitality. Therefore, each individual Jew is greatly in need of community" (*Orot*). Thus Lee was tormented by profound emotional and spiritual anguish. "How can I be part of a community if I can't stand people?" he asked himself.

While watching television footage of a devastating earthquake in Peru, Lee noticed Red Cross volunteers handing out water bottles to the victims. "That's it—I'll be a volunteer! I can be of service to the community and not be expected to speak, since there's a language barrier." Lee promptly registered as a Red Cross volunteer and was soon traveling the world handing out water bottles. He was sent to famines in Africa, tsunamis in Asia, and earthquakes in Central America. Lee had finally found his vocation.

While stationed in the Philippines after a particularly destructive tornado, he was approached by a *New York Times* reporter who had witnessed Lee's recurring presence at such disasters and wondered what motivated him. The newsman sought an interview but was rebuffed. "Can't you see I'm busy? I have no time to talk. I have three crates of water bottles to dispense," Lee growled.

Nevertheless, perceiving the potential for a fascinating glimpse into the psychology of humanitarianism, the reporter was persistent. He managed to collect enough information to publish an article in the *Times* Sunday edition titled "Lee Aaronson: Ambassador to the World." Prominent in the layout were photos of Lee handing out water bottles to survivors of the world's most notorious natural and manufactured disasters. To his surprise and dismay, Lee became a media sensation, being compared to Mahatma Gandhi, the Reverend Dr. Martin Luther King Jr., Mother Teresa, and Abraham Lincoln.

From then on, wherever Lee turned up, he was dogged by the international press begging for an interview. Mothers of all cultures exalted him as a role model, hoping their children might become as famous as Lee employing the holy water bottle. Eventually, as was widely anticipated, he was chosen to receive the Nobel Peace Prize for his humanitarian work.

None of this was pleasing to Lee. "I want to hand out water bottles, and now I have to deal with this crap? And the Nobel Peace Prize yet? My life is a nightmare!" Fortuitously, an ethnic-cleansing campaign was underway in Southeast Asia, and he was summoned to hand out water bottles as refugees crossed the border. Shortly before setting out on the journey, he wrote a letter to the Nobel Committee expressing regret for not attending the award ceremony. The committee responded thus:

> Dear Mr. Aaronson,
>
> Once again, the Nobel Committee members extend our warmest congratulations to you as the Nobel Peace Prize recipient. Although we share your regret that you cannot attend this year's celebration, we deeply appreciate your sense of duty to a higher calling. The active

day-to-day fulfillment of your mission is far more important than any award could ever be. We wish you all the best in your tireless efforts to help alleviate distress around the globe. And because your selflessness is inspired by love, not only for humanity collectively, but indeed for every individual whose life you have touched, we are proud to affirm that you are, and will forever be, our Ambassador to the World.

Sincerely,
The Norwegian Nobel Committee
Oslo, Norway

The Suit

"Ethan, is there any chance you can visit us this weekend?" his mother asked. "I don't know what to do with your father. All he wants is sit and watch television. I can't even get him to go out to lunch."

"I'll see what I can do," Ethan answered. "I'm tied up this weekend, but let me see about next week."

"Please. I'm at my wits' end."

It was six months since Harry Levin had retired. He had owned and operated a small clothing store for forty-three years in a working-class section of Philadelphia. He would have continued working if not for diabetes, which caused his hands to tingle and reduced his walking to a crawl. He missed the business, but it wasn't on account of money. His home and commercial property had been paid off, his son was now a successful corporate attorney in New York, and his daily needs were few. No, it was the contact with customers he regretted losing: the kibitzing and the opportunity to tell his long-winded jokes they respectfully endured.

Harry sold the property to a Hispanic family, who converted it to a grocery store. Still, on many mornings he got dressed, downed a cup of coffee, and drove to the location as he had always done. There, he sat in the car and watched the shoppers, many of whom he had known for years, enter and leave. Aware of his torment, his wife dutifully played along.

Ethan arrived on a Saturday afternoon and found his father watching a meaningless football game. After the customary greetings, Ethan began, "Dad, I need a suit. I thought you could help me. Let's go to Man's World and have a look."

Harry lit up. "A suit?"

"Yeah, something for court. Mine are getting old, worn out."

"Why didn't you tell me? I would have gone yesterday to see what they got."

"It just hit me as I was boarding the train."

"That's a great idea," his mother added. "I'll have dinner ready by the time you get back."

Harry was expansive at the store. Delighted to be back in his element, he peppered the salesman with questions about the fabric, the lining, the stitching, and even the buttons. After trying nearly a half dozen suits, they settled on a navy blue on sale for one hundred fifty dollars. Back home, Harry remained buoyant.

"Honey," he shouted out gleefully for his wife as they entered the house, "you've got to see this suit! Ethan, go upstairs and put it on."

Ethan went to his old bedroom, put on the suit, and came back down.

"What did I tell you? Did you ever see such a beautiful suit?" Harry said to his wife.

"Never," she answered affectionately.

"Here, look at the pockets—neat and flat. And the lapels—not stiff like you see in a lot of cheap suits."

"Fantastic!" she exclaimed.

"You want to keep it on?" Harry asked eagerly.

"No, Dad. I'll wear it Monday in court."

Ethan went upstairs and changed back into his original clothes. There was a knock on the door. "Ethan, may I come in?" his mother called softly.

"Sure—come in."

"You did a wonderful thing, dear. I haven't seen your father so happy in months. Thank you."

"I'm glad."

His mother paused, then asked, "You'll never wear that suit, will you?"

"No. It's a cheap, off-the-rack suit. Navy blue yet. Navy bleeds. By this summer, I'll be wearing four shades of blue. I hate to tell you what I pay for suits in New York."

"I can just imagine."

"But it gave him pleasure. That's what I wanted."

On the train back to New York, Ethan reviewed the day. It was so satisfying to see his father happy, even for a short time. Still, as he confided to his mother, he had no intention of wearing the suit. He even contemplated leaving it on the train but decided at the last minute to take it home.

His mother phoned a few days later. "You're going to Melisa's bat mitzvah, right?"

"Of course," Ethan answered. "But I can't make the service. I'll be at the party."

"Ethan, do me a favor. Wear the suit. Your father will be thrilled."

"All right."

Ethan entered the banquet hall wearing the suit and was greeted by his father. "There you are," he crowed. "Now you look like a mensch!" Harry proceeded to parade Ethan around the room, showing off the suit.

"Touch it," Harry invited Morty, who had spent years working in the garment industry. "Did you ever feel such magnificent fabric?"

"Never," Morty replied, glancing at Ethan as if to say, "You're a brave man to wear such a cheap suit."

Ethan was fully aware of what Morty was trying to convey. Nevertheless, the ruse was worth it, as he could see his father's old self, if only for a few hours, coming to life.

Summer Vacation

J une had arrived, and the academic year at Frederick Douglass Elementary School was finally over. Robert, who taught second grade, transferred his personal belongings to his car, bade his colleagues farewell, and drove home. He was weary yet excited since he was about to take an overseas vacation, just as he had done for the past twelve years. Each summer, he traveled to a different region of the globe, such as Central America, Eastern Europe, North Africa, and Russia. This year it was Southeast Asia, which included weeks in Thailand, Cambodia, and Vietnam.

Now eighty-seven years of age, Robert's mother anticipated her son's annual excursions almost as eagerly as he did, for she cherished the opportunity to clean his apartment. "This place is a pigsty. I don't know how you can live here. I can't wait till you leave so I can get to work," she cheerfully reprimanded him each time she visited. This year, in late June, as soon as Robert was on his way to the airport, his mother loaded a bucket with various cleansers, set off for his apartment, and got to work.

It was a labor of love. Her husband had passed away, as had her closest friends. Instead of watching game shows and soap operas on television, cleaning her son's rooms gave her something to look forward to. Now she could proudly assert on the phone, "I can't talk right now. I have a lot to do at Robert's place," rather than endure meaningless, interminable conversation.

Each time Robert returned from his trip, he could predict what he'd see: socks and T-shirts folded smoothly and piled in individual bureau drawers, dress shirts buttoned at the collar and hung unwrinkled in the closet, pants sharply pressed, Venetian blinds dusted, rugs vacuumed, and mail laid out on a table for easy perusal. The bathroom would also be immaculate—both tub and sink descummed, floor mopped, and old rugs replaced. In the kitchen, he'd find the stovetop free of burnt-on residue, faucets polished, dishes

neatly stacked within the cupboard, eating utensils separated, and plastic storage containers arranged by size under the sink. Finally, stains would have been scrubbed from inside the refrigerator, while spoiled food and drinks, as well as expired condiment packets, would have been discarded.

After this year's journey, Robert was glad to be home. It had been a long flight, and he was tired. Making a quick tour of the apartment, he inspected his drawers, closet, and bathroom and found them precisely as expected. Next, he entered the kitchen and, as usual, noted the unblemished top of the gas range, the evenly stacked dishes, the plasticware in size order, and the compartmentalized utensils.

Feeling satisfied but thirsty, he opened the refrigerator and was shocked to see that out-of-date condiment packets had not been tossed, stubborn stains had become indelible, and spoiled food remained in place, undisturbed. Robert stared for nearly a minute, then closed the door, wandered into the living room, sank onto the sofa, and cried.

Confidence
Lov

EMET

Though the Kaplan brothers were raised in a Conservative Jewish home, Morris began drifting toward Orthodox Judaism, while Bob grew increasingly secular, bordering on agnostic, in outlook. Thus, whereas Morris became active in Jewish affairs, served on the executive board of his synagogue, attended Shabbat services both Friday and Saturday, and observed dietary law, Bob displayed little interest in traditional Jewish life. For instance, Bob's daughter had a bat mitzvah that was conducted at a Reform synagogue and led by a lesbian rabbi. Morris disapproved yet said nothing. Indeed, although they both strove to keep religion out of their conversation, it crept in often enough for disharmony.

Just two weeks after the death of their father, Bob phoned Morris. "There's a great deal on wide-screen TVs at Richard's. Come on, let's take a look."

"You know I can't," Morris replied firmly.

"Oh, *that*," Bob groaned.

"That's right—the *sheloshim*. You're not supposed to buy anything extravagant for thirty days after a funeral."

"I suppose that leaves out next week's 76ers game," Bob teased.

Morris was stern. "Why even mention that? You know the rule: no parties, concerts, or any kind of entertainment for thirty days. Ask me again next month."

"Oy," Bob groaned again, now exasperated.

"Look, I'm Orthodox; you're secular. Fine. Try to respect my feelings on these things."

"Bye," Bob snapped, abruptly ending the call: for he was aggrieved by the lack of respect for *his* feelings.

Friction between the brothers was no less likely on those occasions when they agreed to spend time together in person. This was evident when they met for lunch one Tuesday after some weeks without contact.

"How's business?" Morris ventured, temporarily mellowed by the corned beef special.

Bob was enthusiastic enough to put down his pie fork. "Fantastic! Bring in more immigrants, I say. These people haven't a clue how to buy a car. No matter what price I dangle, they bite. The engine's rotted, the tires are worn, it's got lousy gas mileage—but whatever I say, they believe."

Morris was aghast. "So you're cheating them."

"Business is business."

"But you're not honest."

Bob protested, "Who's honest in the auto industry? No one tells the truth. It's the biggest scam in the country. See those TV ads? See any car in a traffic jam? It's all open road."

Morris's face now assumed the grave and patient expression of a sage. "May I say something?"

"Here goes," Bob sighed. "What?"

"The Hebrew word for truth is *emet,* formed by the first letter of the alphabet, *alef;* the middle letter, *mem;* and the final letter, *tav.*"

"What do you mean?"

"I mean that God is truth, and thus to deceive someone is strictly forbidden."

Though on the defensive, Bob gave no ground. "I'm sorry. I have a family to feed. I can't be so moral, especially in my business."

"Keep it in mind. That's all I'm saying. How's Bethany?"

Bob rolled his eyes. "How many times do I have to tell you? Her name's Bettany: b-e-t-t-a-n-y, not Bethany. There's no *h,* and if there were, we'd make it silent."

"It's just that Grandmom's name was Beth."

"So? She got the b-e-t. That's enough. Now she can rest, wherever she is. We like Bettany. It's a cool name—Jewish, but maybe not. Good for her career. Anyway, she's planning a junior year abroad. We're torn between Brazil and Thailand."

"Are those the only two countries to consider?" Morris asked.

"No, there's quite a few."

"May I make a suggestion?"

"Go ahead."

"How about Israel?"

"Oh, you mean New Jersey?"

"*What?*"

"Israel—it's the size of New Jersey. If I'm going to send her to Israel, I might as well send her to Atlantic City."

"But she'd learn about her faith."

"She doesn't need Israel. She eats at Hymie's deli. That's Jewish enough. She wants something exotic."

"It's only a suggestion."

Bob looked at his watch. "Time to go. As usual, another splendid lunch," he said sarcastically. "Tell me something. How in the world were we ever conceived as brothers? We have absolutely nothing in common."

As expected, Bettany chose Brazil. The night before she was to leave, she phoned her uncle. "Hi, Uncle Morris. It's Bettany. Just calling to say goodbye. I'm off to Brazil tomorrow."

"Well, have a great time, but don't forget to study."

"I won't. I'll call you when I get back."

Five months passed, and Bettany flew back home. Bob waited eagerly at the airport, expecting to glow with pride when she appeared. After gathering her bags, Bettany came outside and spotted her father standing beside the car. As she approached, he was shocked to see that her entire body, from neck to foot, was covered with tattoos.

"Bettany," Bob stammered, "how could you do this to yourself?"

"Aren't they beautiful? Look, I have a heart on my arm with 'Tommy' in the middle. He's my new boyfriend."

"Bettany, Jews should not be getting tattoos. There's even something in the Torah about that."

"In the what?" Bettany asked.

The Better Life

It would be hard to imagine two brothers with less in common than Brad and Lenny Crouse. Whereas Brad was generally quiet and reserved, Lenny was noisy and gregarious. And while Brad was academically inclined early on, winning numerous achievement awards, Lenny took scant interest in scholarship, preferring to perform for any audience he could attract. In fact, relatives frequently visited the Crouse home on Sunday evenings, where Lenny sang and danced to the musical themes of popular television shows such as *The Beverly Hillbillies*, *Green Acres*, and *Happy Days*. Throughout these entertainments, Brad would sit attentively, admiring Lenny's talent albeit with a touch of jealousy.

During high school, these distinctions became even more pronounced. While Brad developed a deep interest in the natural sciences, especially chemistry and biology, Lenny precociously gained near-celebrity status, winning the leading role in almost every musical production. At the same time, he had become well known as one of the city's top tap-dancers.

In his senior year, Brad was accepted to the University of Pennsylvania. A year later, it was Lenny's time to choose. His grades were, at least, good enough to enter a state college. It thus came as a shock to his parents when he decided to skip college and move to New York to pursue a career in the performing arts.

"You want to be a singer, a dancer? Fine. I'm not saying don't do it," his father advised. "But you need a fallback plan. Get a teaching degree. You can still perform, but at least you'll have a steady job."

"Dad, I'm not like Brad. I can't sit still and read books. I need activity—I must connect. I'm moving to New York."

Following graduation from high school, Lenny took a bus to New York and began auditioning for plays, musicals, and even television commercials. When Brad graduated from Penn, he enrolled in the medical school at Johns Hopkins University, specializing in endocrinology. At about this time, Lenny got his first major break, winning the part of Lancelot in the Broadway revival of Lerner and Lowe's *Camelot*. This led to other coveted roles, such as Hap in *Death of a Salesman*, Juan Perón in *Evita*, and Riff in *West Side Story*. Finally, he captured the crown jewel of the Broadway stage, playing Harold Hill in the highly anticipated revival of *The Music Man*.

And yet, despite his success, there was one thing Lenny desired above all else. He wanted his brother to acknowledge that he, Lenny, had the better life, that he was willing to do what his brother lacked the courage to do: take a chance. He wanted Brad to admit having chosen the *easy* path—to study and advance through well-defined steps to become a doctor, while Lenny had the inner strength to defy their father and follow his dream.

Lenny invited his brother and his wife to opening night for *The Music Man*. Afterward, he met them in the lobby, where they were mobbed by fans seeking Lenny's autograph or a picture taken with him. Despite the constant interruptions, Brad made sure to offer congratulations. "You were magnificent. You brought a real freshness to the part."

"You think so?" Lenny responded gratefully.

"Absolutely."

"I only wish Mom and Dad were alive to see this. It was Pop's favorite musical."

"I know. Remember when he sang "Till There Was You" at your bar mitzvah?"

"You call that singing?" Lenny joked. They all chuckled pleasantly.

Driving home, Brad was silent. "Dear, why are you so quiet? You haven't said a word. Is anything wrong?" his wife asked anxiously.

"Nothing," Brad reassured her. But as they approached their home, he suddenly pulled over to the curb. "Marci, there's something I need to say."

"What is it?"

"My brother has the better life."

"How can you say that? You're a doctor."

"No, he has a better life. He defied our father, which I could never do. He followed his dream and became a success."

"You followed your dream, too."

"Not like him. I just followed a script. 'You wanna be a doctor? Here's how you do it.' There's no risk in that. But he took a chance. He had the guts. He moved to New York at nineteen, bounced around for years, and eventually made it. Now he's famous and well respected, and I'm sure has a few bucks in his pocket."

"So do you."

Brad laughed. "The bottom line is this: he has the better life. Now you must promise me something."

"What?"

"Never, even after I'm gone, are you to tell Lenny or anyone else what I just said. Do you promise?"

"Yes."

"Good. Let's go home."

LIFE ON MARS

Paul Rosenberg was a world-famous astrophysicist who served as a consultant to the National Aeronautics and Space Administration (NASA). He also regularly contributed scholarly papers to leading scientific journals. But Paul's main focus was developing a specialized telescope for viewing life on Mars. Finally, after many years of painstaking trial and error, it was ready.

Yet what would typically bring a profound sense of accomplishment brought Paul only misery and regret, for among his discoveries was a colony of Jews who were either ignorant or utterly dismissive of *Halakhah*— Jewish law. For example, they observed Sabbath on Wednesdays; Yom Kippur was an occasion for binge eating; and outlet malls had names such as The Promised Land. Not able to tolerate such abominations, Paul had the telescope destroyed.

Even so, the telescopic revelations never entirely left Paul's consciousness, as evidenced by his scribbling in the margins of various publications notes such as "Yom Kippur buffet—children under 12 free" and "Take your family to The Promised Land—buses leave every half hour." When colleagues inquired about these mysterious fragments, he maintained a Sphinx-like silence. And though students continue to study Paul's masterful scholarly works, by the time of his death there had developed an intense interest in the scribbled annotations, with the result that, to this day, national organizations compete to solve what has become known as Rosenberg's Riddle.

APPENDIX

A Unique Feature of the Rosenberg Telescope

The telescope was equipped with a microphone that enabled the researcher to hear extraterrestrial conversation. The voice recordings were given to a battery of linguists, who succeeded in deciphering only one exchange, as follows:

Speaker A: What's your name?

Speaker B: 4829573. What's your name?

Speaker A: 8296295.

Speaker B: That's funny. You don't look Jewish.

Potential Implications for Anthropology and Iconology

In addition to the departure from religious behavioral norms, Paul noticed that Martian Jews had horns, leading him to speculate that Michelangelo may have had contact with the tribe before creating the Moses statue. This poses a challenge to the traditional iconological argument that a biblical verse inspired the horns: "And when Moses came down from Mount Sinai, he held the two tablets of the testimony, and he knew not that his face was horned from the conversation of the Lord" (Exodus 34:29).

An Unfortunate Lapse in Judgment

Rosenberg came to regret destroying the telescope, having learned that raising money for charitable purposes was just as important as observing Torah laws. "Had I known," he confessed, "I would never have destroyed both the telescope and the highly complex instructions for assembling it. Who knows what I might have witnessed—perhaps a bric-a-brac auction, or even a Jerry Lewis–type telethon."

A Riddle for the Ages

Rosenberg's Riddle calls to mind Fermat's Theorem, formulated by the French mathematician Pierre de Fermat, which took 358 years to solve (1637–1994). It is predicted that the solution to Rosenberg's Riddle will take much longer.

The Garden of Eating

Oh, how Gene and Myrna Schultz loved to eat! Tasty food, and plenty of it, was the glue that held their marriage together, a respite from their otherwise constant bickering. Each week in their rollercoaster relationship, the high point was to dine on Saturday night at Great Wall Chinese Buffet, where they feasted on such mutual favorites as spareribs, sweet-and-sour chicken, beef with broccoli, and spring rolls.

It thus came as a shock one evening when they were greeted by a hand-lettered sign on the restaurant window: CLOSE FOR TWO WEEKS. WILL REOPEN ON APRIL 11. On the verge of a panic attack, Gene immediately confronted the owner, Mr. Chin. "Why are you closing? How can you do this to us?"

Mr. Chin bowed politely. "Good luck occasion. My daughter in China get married. So sorry to you."

The Schultzes were at a loss where to eat the following Saturday, as they had been going exclusively to Great Wall for nearly eight years. When Gene suggested they try another Chinese buffet, Myrna immediately objected, chirping shrilly, "No way. Nothing could replace Great Wall." Sensing that a dispute was brewing, they stayed home and sulked over a shared can of split pea soup.

Gene complained to a colleague at work about their plight. "Try The Garden of Eden," he offered. "They have a buffet that would shame a bar mitzvah." However, being more aware of Gene's urgent need than of his generally conservative nature, the colleague failed to mention that The Garden of Eden was the city's premier adult swingers club.

Saturday arrived, and the Schultzes set out with high hopes for The Garden of Eden. As they crossed the threshold, a host intercepted them. "First-timers?" he asked, after quickly taking their measure.

"Yes," replied Gene.

"Let me explain what we have. First, as you can see over there, we have a full-course buffet. Eat as much as you like."

"That's why we're here," Myrna replied eagerly.

"I see your wife has a sense of humor," the host continued, studying Gene's reaction. "Now, in the basement, we have what we call the Medieval Room. It has a rack and a guillotine for those who, shall we say, like it dark."

"I don't understand," said Myrna.

"Myrna," Gene groaned with exasperation, "do I have to explain *everything*? The 'rack' is rack of lamb—a delicacy, by the way, that we never found at Great Wall. The 'guillotine' is the carving station, and 'dark' refers to dark meat like beef or liver. Geez!"

The host did not bat an eye. "May I continue?"

"Please, go ahead," Gene replied.

"Upstairs, we have rooms for couples."

"Private dining," responded Myrna, her confidence reviving.

"We also have a large room where anyone can enter," the host added.

Gene nodded approvingly. "Wonderful—community dining."

"I do hope it's family-style," added Myrna.

On the way home, they were overjoyed—not to mention overfed. "I never ate so well," belched Gene.

"Same here," sighed Myrna. "I think they should change the name from The Garden of Eden to The Garden of Eating." They laughed companionably at Myrna's play on words.

"Everyone was so friendly!" Gene exclaimed. "We met so many couples who invited us to their homes!"

"We have their phone numbers. We'll have to visit them sometimes," replied Myrna.

"Absolutely!" responded Gene.

During the second Saturday dinner, it dawned on the Schultzes that The Garden of Eden was a swingers club, and they became active members. The Chins returned to the United States refreshed by their family's happiness and promptly reopened the restaurant with an enhanced menu. However, they never saw Gene and Myrna again, much to their dismay and bewilderment.

THE PERFECT LIFE

Although Judaism is not overly concerned with the afterlife, Myer Kornfeld was consumed by this mystery early on—that is, as soon as he had attained the age of reason. Indeed, he dwelt on it to the exclusion of nearly every other line of thought. What happens after you die? Do you go to heaven or spend eternity in hell? were questions that had monopolized his consciousness for years. Although he came short of uncovering definitive answers, he chose to follow a strict diet, exercise regularly, and even color his hair as it turned greyer. "After all," he considered, "it's important to make a good impression when meeting your maker."

Now approaching eighty, Myer surveyed his past and was gratified to conclude that he had lived the perfect life. For example, he had never told a lie—no, not even a minor fib for the sake of a major advantage; had never cheated anyone; and had never injured or killed anyone or anything—except, he admitted, for the occasional mosquito. Thus, Myer was confident he was slated for a blissful existence in heaven.

However, this condition of serenity was bound to be disrupted. One day, while Myer was sitting at peace on a park bench, a disturbing thought invaded his mind. He suddenly remembered that he had stolen a small bag of candy corn from a grocery store near his home as a second-grader. Though the price was only five cents, the memory of it caused him countless sleepless nights. "How can I get into heaven if I don't make amends?" he asked himself, trembling. He recalled that the grocery store was owned by an Abe Grossman and imagined meeting him in the afterlife.

"Well, if it isn't the little candy corn thief, Myer Kornfeld! I knew I was short one bag when I took inventory. Then it occurred to me how suspicious you looked when you left the store."

To calm his mind, Myer decided to see a play. But Shakespeare's *Macbeth* only increased his agitation, especially when, referring to her involvement in the murder of King Duncan, Lady Macbeth cried, "Will all great Neptune's ocean wash this blood / Clean from my hand?" In Myer's judgment, the pilfering of the candy ranked with the killing of Duncan in terms of gravity and the call for remorse.

He hired a private investigator to locate Abe Grossman. A few months later, he was informed that both Abe and his wife, Ruth, had passed away. However, their daughter, Rachel, was teaching English at Jake's Happy English School in the Gobi Desert along the Mongolia-China border. Myer immediately flew to Ulan Bator, Mongolia's capital, and joined a two-week caravan through the Gobi. After enduring considerable hardship, he stood face to face with Rachel Grossman and related his mission.

"You traveled seven thousand miles to tell me some mashugana[5] story about a bag of candy corn? You're out of your mind."

"It's of the utmost importance to me," Myer responded, urgently yet matter-of-factly. "I've done some calculations, and figure five cents in 1952 is worth about a dollar and a half today." He pulled a tattered dollar bill and two grimy quarters from his pocket. "Please, take it. I beg you, take it."

"And if I don't?" she challenged.

"Then I'll stand here until you do."

Rachel reluctantly accepted the money, allowing Myer to return, unburdened, to the United States. Upon reaching home, he received a phone call from his daughter.

"Where were you?" she demanded. "I was worried sick, leaving you message after message. Nobody knew where you were."

"I went to Mongolia."

"What the hell were you doing in Mongolia?"

Myer patiently recounted his adventure. She sought to have him committed, but too much paperwork was required. Thus, Myer was free to resume his disciplined habits—diet, exercise, and an occasional touch-up.

---

5.   **Mashugana:** Crazy, insane.

All told, between the private investigator, the round-trip airfare to Mongolia, the two-week caravan to meet Rachel, and the two-week journey back to Ulan Bator, as well as food and lodging, he had spent close to $50,000 to restore a dollar and a half. Nevertheless, Myer felt no regret about the expense, because now there was no doubt he had lived the perfect life.

The Joke

Larry Blatt had made it. After years of trying his luck at open mics, driving as far as fifty miles to do a five-minute set, he had finally gained traction in his comedy career, performing at elite comedy clubs and casinos in both the United States and Canada. He not only had mastered the art of telling jokes, but had become adept as an impressionist, imitating such luminaries as Robert De Niro, Al Pacino, and Christopher Walken. The audience would quip that you came to see not only Larry but other celebrities as well.

Larry was scheduled for a three-night run at Giggles, Philadelphia's premier comedy club. He phoned his brother Ira and sister-in-law Harriet, who lived in Radnor, a Philadelphia suburb, and invited them to the Saturday night performance. They readily accepted. "Thanks, we'll certainly be there," Ira said.

"Come backstage after the show," Larry added.

"Of course. We haven't seen you for a while."

"That's show business—never a free moment."

"Listen, Larry, we have some good news of our own."

"What's that?"

"Jennifer's getting married!"

Larry was surprised and delighted. "For real?"

"Yes!"

"To the med student?"

"That's right."

"Nice young man. And very smart. Did you set a date?"

"Sunday, May 23. Of course, we hope you can make it."

"Let me check my calendar. Just a moment." Larry soon returned. "No problem. I'm performing in Chicago that Saturday, but I'll take an early flight Sunday. Hey, I'll even entertain. I'll put together 'bout ten minutes."

"Terrific! Hold on. Talk to Harriet." He handed her the phone.

"You'll do ten minutes?" Harriet asked.

"Absolutely. And congratulations—you may be grandparents someday."

"From your lips," Harriet replied.

"Could you put Ira back on?" Larry asked.

"Here I am," Ira said.

"I gotta run. See you Saturday. Your tickets will be held at the box office."

"We'll be there. Looking forward to it."

Saturday night was a packed house at Giggles. Many fans held Larry's latest CD, hoping to get his autograph. Peeping through the curtain, Larry spotted his brother and sister-in-law sitting front-row center. After two warm-up comedians, the Master of Ceremonies took the mic. "Time for our headliner, back from a highly successful week at the MGM Grand in Las Vegas. You've seen him on *Late Night* and *Comedy Central*, and he'll soon be making a movie with the one-and-only Robin Williams. Here he is, a Philadelphia native— let's give a warm welcome to tonight's and every night's headliner, Larry Blatt!"

Larry entered to a long and noisy standing ovation. He began by thanking the audience for the love and support they had given him through his lean years, then launched into his act. He reminisced about

growing up in Kensington, a tough working-class Philadelphia neighborhood where being Jewish was challenging. He fondly described his mother, who never said a bad word about anyone ("You know, Saddam Hussein without the mustache was a very good-looking man!"). And, of course, he wowed the crowd with his impressions, all the while taking in his brother's approving smile.

Toward the end of his act, Larry mentioned that he had just turned sixty and observed how the world was suddenly treating him differently. "Now, when I call for a taxi, an ambulance arrives. But the worst thing is when I'm with my eight-year-old niece because, in her eyes, I'm ancient. She said to me, 'What did you do today, Uncle Larry?' I replied, 'I went shopping.' She goes, 'You went shopping? Did you carry your bags, or did someone carry them for you?' I carried the bags . . . bitch." That's my time. Thank you, and good night."

Again, Larry received a thunderous standing ovation. He was taking off his makeup when his brother and sister-in-law entered the dressing room. He saw them through the mirror, stood up, and gave each a hug. "What did you think?"

"Fantastic," Ira answered. "The stuff about Mom was spot-on. Very funny."

Larry then turned to Harriet. "Did you like it?"

"It was wonderful," answered Harriet. She paused. "Except for one thing."

"What's that?" asked Larry.

"The last joke," responded Harriet.

Larry was taken aback. "What last joke?"

Harriet's face tightened. "You called our daughter a bitch."

"What?!"

"That last joke—you talked about your niece; then you called her a bitch."

"I did *not* say anything about your daughter. The girl in the joke is eight years old!" exclaimed Larry in amazement. "How old is Jennifer?"

"Twenty-seven," Harriet answered.

"You see, it's not your daughter. They're two separate people."

"But you specifically referred to your niece, and you have only one niece—who happens to be our daughter."

Larry turned to his brother. "Ira, do you feel the same way?"

"Well, maybe you can find another joke," Ira suggested cautiously.

"I can't. It's my closer. You heard how the audience laughed."

"I'm just telling you how I feel," said Harriet firmly. "I would appreciate it, and I think Ira would agree, if you didn't use that joke again. You've been a comedian for many years. I'm sure you can find another— what's that word again, the thing that ends a show?"

"Closer."

"Right. Closer. Anyway, we have to get going."

"It was great seeing you," Ira put in diplomatically. "Good luck tomorrow night."

"Yeah, thanks," Larry said irritably. "Drive safely."

A month passed. Ira called Larry, who was now filming in Hollywood with Robin Williams. "How's everything in La La Land?" Ira asked.

"Great. Robin's a pleasure to work with, very professional. How you been?"

"Busy. Tax time's coming," answered Ira, who was an accountant.

"I can understand that. Well, you know how to handle it."

"Look, Larry, I hope you don't mind my asking but are you still using that joke about the niece?"

"Ira, you're an accountant. In a million years, I wouldn't tell you how to perform your job. Likewise, you ought not tell me how to perform mine. To answer your question: yes, I'm using that joke. I did a show

two nights ago, and the audience roared. That's my job—making people laugh. The minute the laughter stops, I'm back busing tables at Irv's Deli."

"Just asking—nothing to get upset about. Well, give my best to Robin."

"Goodbye," answered Larry coldly.

Another month passed, and Larry received a call from his niece, Jennifer. "Uncle Larry, it's Jennifer."

"Jennifer! So happy to hear from you, and congratulations on your engagement. I'm sure you'll have a wonderful life together."

"Thank you. I'm thrilled."

"So you're getting married next month. Am I right?"

"That's right."

"I still haven't received my invitation. Do you have my address?"

"We have it."

"Then why haven't I received it?"

"That's why I'm calling. I'm sorry to tell you, but you're not invited. I want you to come, but it's my mother—something to do with a joke."

 Larry reacted with surprise. "What are you talking about?"

"My mother said you told a joke about me that she didn't like, so you're not invited to the wedding. I want you to come—but you know my mother. Once she makes up her mind, there's no persuading her."

"First of all, the joke was not about you. It was about my make-believe niece, who is eight years old. And second, I can't believe because of a joke I'm not invited to your wedding. It's ridiculous."

"Uncle Larry, I'm so sorry. I want you to know I feel terrible, but that's how my mother is. That's why my father called you last month. We were all listening to see if you were still telling the joke, and when you said yes, my mother decided not to invite you."

"This breaks my heart."

"Mine too."

"And your father agrees?"

"I don't think so. He tried to reason with her, but he couldn't get anywhere. Like I said, once she makes up her mind . . ."

Larry sighed sadly. "Listen, dear, I'll still send a check."

"Thank you."

"Give my best to everyone at your wedding."

"I will."

The next day Larry called Ira. "Are you alone?" Larry asked.

"Yes," replied Ira.

"I'm now going to say something to you I've never said before."

"What?"

"Fuck you! You hear me? Fuck you! Can't you defend me just one time in your shit marriage?"

"Watch it!"

"I will not watch it, and if you hang up, you'll never hear from me again."

"I tried. Believe me. I tried," pleaded Ira.

"I'm your brother, asshole! Fight for me once in your life."

"What can I do? You know how she is. She gets hysterical."

"She'll get over it."

"No, she won't. I'll be hearing about it the rest of my life."

"I already made the plane reservation."

"I'll pay you back."

"Never mind—I can afford it."

Larry waited until the morning of the wedding, hoping to get a last-minute invitation. It never came, and he did not speak to his brother for two years. But one day, he called Ira. "Listen, I'm back at Giggles next weekend. I'd like both of you to come Saturday evening like the other time. And just to let you know, I'm not using that joke anymore. I have all-new material."

"Larry, I'm so relieved and pleased to hear from you. Let's put all that behind us, okay? Of course, we'll be there. We wouldn't miss it," said Ira happily.

"Tickets will be at the box office. Show starts at ten."

"Thanks. We'll be there."

As before, Ira and Harriet were seated front-row center. Larry took the stage and, for forty minutes, presented jokes and impressions. The last five minutes were devoted to a streak of bad luck he had been experiencing with dating, airport security, hospitals, and restaurants.

"But," Larry concluded, "through it all, I have developed one very useful quality: I can hide my true feelings. For example, to this day, my brother—raise your hand, Ira." Ira raised his hand. "To this day— ready for this?—my brother thinks I love him."

Daddy Issues

Isaac Krumholtz, a sprightly yet somewhat reclusive seventy-four-year-old, attended the wedding celebration of his granddaughter, Emily. For the feast, he was seated with friends and relatives of similar age. Making the rounds with her new husband, Emily stopped at their table, thanked everyone for coming, then addressed Isaac. "Grandpop, you lived in Japan, didn't you?"

"Yes. I taught English there in the 1970s. Why do you ask?"

"I have a friend who's going to Japan for her junior year. She's looking for someone who can tell her firsthand about the country's culture and maybe help her with basic vocabulary for conversation."

"Where is she?"

Emily pointed across the room. "She's over there. Come with me. I'll introduce you."

Isaac followed his granddaughter to a table populated by young women, none of whom, he guessed, was more than twenty-five years of age. "Sandy," Emily said, "this is my grandfather. He lived in Japan. How many years, Grandpop?"

"Eight," Isaac answered.

"Sandy, I told him you were planning to study there, so perhaps you two could meet, and he could help you prepare."

"That would be wonderful," Sandy responded, eyes sparkling. "Would you have any time for us to get together, Mister . . . ?"

"The name's Krumholtz, but please call me Isaac. Sure, no problem. I'm retired, so I have plenty of time."

"Could you give me your phone number? I'll call you tomorrow evening if that's okay."

"Fine. I'm usually up late," he lied.

Isaac dug a pen from his pocket. Sandy scavenged a scrap of paper from her cluttered handbag, and Isaac jotted down his number.

"I'll bet you can you tell I'm apprehensive. I've never been anywhere, and Japan seems so alien—exotic," Sandy said, her voice hinting at nervousness.

Isaac enjoyed reassuring her. "It is, but the Japanese are cordial to Americans. You shouldn't have any problem."

"Let me return to my friends. We can talk tomorrow."

They shook hands, and when Isaac was back at his table, he was not sure whether he had walked or floated on the way. He had never seen nor spoken to a woman as beautiful as Sandy—perfect figure; long black hair; an infectious smile; and soft, delicate hands. Isaac could barely sleep that night, nor could he eat the following day. He canceled a couple of long-awaited medical appointments to practice what he'd say when she called. The anxiety became so intense that he almost wished she *wouldn't* call.

From seven o'clock that evening, he sat on a couch, motionless, staring at the phone. The kitchen clock ticked mercilessly. By eleven o'clock, already two hours past his bedtime, he reasoned that, indeed, she wouldn't call. "Look at me," he admonished himself. "An alter kocker[6] thinking I could have a chance with such a divine creature. She's probably making love to some muscle-bound galoot and forgot all about it."

At 11:30, the phone rang. "Hello, Isaac, this is Sandy. I hope it's not too late. I was studying and lost all track of time."

"That's okay. I usually don't get to sleep till two in the morning," he lied again.

"Glad to hear it! I have an uncle around your age who goes to bed at nine—can you believe?"

---

6. **Alter kocker:** Older adult, old-timer.

"That's ridiculous," Isaac answered without missing a beat.

"Anyway, as Emily explained, I'm heading off to Japan in a few weeks and just thought you could tell me how it was for you there, maybe teach me a few Japanese words, so I don't give the impression of a complete idiot."

"I'd be happy to. I even know some people who can show you around. They're Japanese, but they speak good English."

"That would be wonderful. We could meet at a Starbucks, say, this Sunday afternoon. Does that work for you?"

"What time?"

"Around two o'clock. Let's meet at the one at 18th and Spruce."

"I'll be there."

Dazed, Isaac hung up the phone, changed into his pajamas, put out the lights, and fainted at the foot of the bed. It had been nearly ten years since he was intimate with a woman. It was with Sylvia Pearlstein, who must have weighed around three hundred pounds and had a personality to match. The encounter was a disaster, as Isaac had difficulty maintaining an erection. By evening's end, he had wrecked eight condoms and wasted half a tube of lubricating gel before giving up. Though he had concluded his sex life was over, he nevertheless kept the remaining condoms and the half-used lubricating gel in the glove compartment of his car as a memento of a more vigorous time and condition.

On the appointed day, Sandy and Isaac met at Starbucks and carried their coffee upstairs to talk. They chatted for nearly two hours as he introduced her to Japanese customs, recommended places to visit, and taught her the most useful words and phrases.

"Is there anything else you would like to know?" Isaac inquired politely.

"I think we covered the essentials. For the rest, I simply need to go there."

"That's right—nothing like a real-life experience."

"Thank you so much. Listen, since you've been so kind, I'd like to treat you to dinner."

"You don't have to," Isaac protested mildly, pinching himself under the table.

"Please. I want to repay you for all your help. I was thinking of next Saturday night. Do you know Gino's on Old York Road? I love it there. Say, around seven?"

"Seven it is," Isaac agreed, now drawing blood.

"Great! Well, I have to get back to my studies. See you Saturday." When she was out of view, Isaac asked the barista for a Band-Aid.

They met at Gino's as planned, but Sandy was quiet throughout the meal, unlike her liveliness during their previous meeting. Isaac became concerned that he was boring her. "Is everything all right? You've hardly said a word."

Sandy began hesitatingly, "There *is* something . . . I need to tell you."

"What's that?"

She sighed, "I have daddy issues."

Isaac almost sighed, too—with relief. "Look, that's normal. I never had a good relationship with my father. I remember how it was growing up. All we did was fight."

Sandy's face lit up with one of those smiles he admired. "Isaac, that's not what 'daddy issues' means. It means I'm attracted to older men."

"Oh!" gulped Isaac, who would have pinched himself were last week's wound not still healing.

"And there's something else I must tell you. The story about Japan is fiction. It was just a way to meet you. Emily was aware of my interest in older men. She also knew you had lived in Japan, so we pretended I was going there. I'm sorry I deceived you."

Isaac felt a flash of annoyance, but it quickly left. "It's okay," he responded smoothly. "I understand."

"Now that you know the truth, I want you to be honest. Do you like me?"

"Of course. Do *you* like *me?*"

"Isaac, are you blind? I'm madly in love with you! Let's not bother finishing our meal. Let's go to my place, right now. You can follow me."

Isaac paid the bill and drove to Sandy's building. Before exiting the car he removed the four remaining condoms and the half tube of lubricating gel from the glove compartment.

As soon as they entered the apartment, they kissed while undressing each other. Naked, they went to her bed, where they continued kissing and caressing.

"I assume you want me to use a condom," Isaac stated matter-of-factly.

"Yes, if you don't mind. Better we don't take any chances."

Isaac stood up to retrieve the condoms and lubricating gel from his pants pocket. Returning to the bed, he showed her the gel. "Do you need this?" he asked.

"You dirty old man," she cooed. "Just look at you. You've already used half the gel!"

Isaac stared at the tube and was jolted into a memory of the long-ago evening with Sylvia Pearlstein. Then, gazing at Sandy's body, he burst into laughter at the contrast. And try as he might, he couldn't stop the eruption. With tears streaming down his cheeks, he fled to the bathroom, struggling to control himself. But the laughter only grew more violent as Sandy looked on in helpless amazement.

Climbing back into bed, exhausted, Isaac was still unable to halt the paroxysms. But suddenly he became silent, drew in a deep breath, and collapsed onto the floor. Rushing to his side, Sandy could see that Isaac had stopped breathing and called 9-1-1. A team of medics arrived and attempted to restart his heart, but it was too late. Isaac had literally died laughing.

As required for the record, the medical crew questioned Sandy. In shock, and thus not thinking clearly, she volunteered, indiscriminately, every step and detail, from the moment when they first met at the wedding, to her daddy issues, to the Japan ruse, to the kissing and undressing, and finally to the fatal laughing fit. Alas, one less-than-scrupulous medic posted the entire transcript on Facebook, revealing names and addresses as well as displaying photographs for the curious.

Within hours, nearly the entire literate and media-savvy population, throughout both hemispheres, had read or heard the sad story. Sandy became—in a word—radioactive, as no man would approach her for fear of dropping dead in the manner of Isaac Krumholtz. "Hell if I'm going to die laughing," otherwise bullish young studs would bellow.

The notoriety and embarrassment became such that Sandy flew to Nepal, where she has recently been spotted herding yaks in a remote section of the Himalayas. Ironically, the plane made a brief stop in Japan en route.

Sound Advice

Asher loved his father unconditionally—animal instinct and human nature sufficed to ensure that much. But when he was old enough to appreciate the blessings in their relationship, he realized that he regarded his father not only as a progenitor but also as a mentor: a companion, a guide, his wiser friend. As Asher grew up, his father led him through various activities and experiences to build the boy into a man and introduce him to the world he would inhabit. Together they camped without amenities in the wilder depths of national parks; inspected historic monuments; sang in an all-male chorus; participated in volunteer work; and, as a counterpoint, indulged just once in a visit to Disney World. Along the way, his father exemplified such values as truthfulness in everyday matters, fairness to others, and kindness to all living things.

And yet, there was one guideline that Asher found troubling. His father had instructed that he should quit without hesitation if he were ever unhappy with a job. But, unfortunately, this advice flew in the face of what Asher considered an essential American trait: the ability to withstand adversity—stick-to-it-iveness, as his compatriots liked to call it. In fact, at more than one place of employment, he saw posted the poem "Don't Quit" by John Greenleaf Whittier, which included the following lines:

> So stick to the fight when you're hardest hit
> It's when things seem worst that you must not quit.

Nevertheless, he took to heart his father's counsel and left each job as soon as he experienced the first pangs of dissatisfaction: a habit that, over time, became an issue. Eventually, Asher summoned the courage to question his father. "Dad, I love and honor you, but your advice about quitting is causing me problems.

Interviewers are surprised to see how many jobs I've had in so short a period. Employers consider me unreliable."

"I understand how you feel, son," his father answered firmly. "But trust me. I know what I'm saying. Someday you will thank me."

Thus Asher continued to bounce from one situation to the next until he found a position he believed was a keeper: stock analyst for a brokerage firm in New York City's financial district. He flourished in this role for a year—but one day, without warning, he was overwhelmed by an uncanny urge to quit. His father's devoted son as ever, he promptly resigned.

Asher visited his father's grave a week later and gently placed a small rock upon the stone. After a silent meditation, he knelt and thanked his father. For Asher had worked inside the World Trade Center until September 10, 2001, the day before the towers were destroyed.

STEPHANIE

Stephanie was raised—if not born—to be a princess. And not a contemporary, enlightened, down-to earth princess, but more on the model of a despotic storybook princess whose every whim must be satisfied without question, on pain of banishment—or perhaps even worse. For example, if she lost or broke a possession of great or slight value, it was soon replaced without rebuke, as her parents wished her life to be as carefree as possible. There was a younger brother with autism, and although his parents spared no expense in providing therapy and general care, their emotional love and encouragement were primarily invested in Stephanie. "At least we have one normal child," they would reassure each other privately.

Throughout her preteen and teenage years, Stephanie conducted herself following her notion of royalty— she was vain, inconsiderate, and arrogant, with her parents as willing consorts. If, for example, she suddenly felt the urge to tour Spain, first-class reservations would be booked. If she fancied herself a singer, dancer, or musician, private lessons would be arranged. And if she required the most advanced technological device on its initial day of sale, her father would take off work to stand in line for hours on her behalf.

When it was time to apply for college, Stephanie insisted on an expensive out-of-state four-year liberal arts school, though her parents had tried to convince her to settle for a local state university where the tuition was considerably more affordable. Even when away from home, she continued to indulge in her habitual carelessness with material goods, which were unquestioningly replaced. To make matters worse, Stephanie frequently changed apartments, as her roommates could not tolerate her selfish and willful behavior.

After Stephanie's four less-than-exemplary years, her parents were proud and relieved to witness the graduation ceremony. The family returned home together, but Stephanie quickly retreated to her old

bedroom. She lost no time in resuming her favorite activity—multitasking as she communicated with friends on the latest pieces of technological wizardry. But soon there was a knock on the door.

"Stephanie, it's your father. May I come in?"

"Just a moment. I'm texting someone."

Accustomed to patience, her father waited outside her room for five minutes. "Stephanie, may I come in now?"

"Oh, you still there?" she groaned, annoyed. "Okay, come in, but not too long. I'm busy."

Her father entered and was dismayed as she continued to talk on her phone and chat on the computer. "Stephanie, I need to speak with you."

"My God!" Stephanie snapped. "Can't you see I'm swamped? What is it? Make it fast."

Her father responded mildly, "It's just that your mother and I wonder what your plans are now that you've graduated."

"You're looking at it."

"What?"

"Are you deaf? I said you're looking at it."

"What do you mean?"

With insolent matter-of-factness, Stephanie explained, "I mean, I plan to stay home, play on the computer, eat your food, go shopping, meet friends for lunch, and travel on your dime. Do you have a problem with that?"

Her father persisted: "How about a job or graduate school? It's wise to plan for your future."

She ranted, "That *is* my future. Are you serious—a *job*? Do you think I should waste my best years in some boring office? And for what? You have money. Why do I have to make money? And graduate school? Let

me tell you something, Lou." (It had been a long time since she had called him "Dad.") "I'm not trained to do anything."

"You have a college degree," her father countered.

"Listen, you know the checks you sent me whenever I said something was lost or broken?"

"Yes?"

"Wasn't true. I used the money to bribe grad students to write my papers. Of course, the dean became suspicious, but you were paying full tuition, so why kill the golden goose? And why should *I* work? Sally never worked." (It had been a long time since she had called her mother "Mom.")

Her father was taken aback. "That's different. We're married."

"Hey, that's a good idea. Maybe I can marry some schmuck like you and live off *his* dime. Thanks, Lou. And one more thing while you're here—keep that weirdo away from me."

"Who?"

"That thing I'm told is my brother."

Her father protested, "That's not right. He *is* your brother, and he has problems."

"Problems?!" Stephanie snorted. "He's a walking freak show. Okay—maybe when no one's here, I'll look at him. But if I have friends over, hide him in the closet or something. Anything else? Tell me now, 'cause I've got things to do."

"No." Grimly silent, he left the room and made his way downstairs. He met his wife in the kitchen and related the conversation with Stephanie. They then decided to do what they had always done—say nothing.

The Brand

Harris Finkel taught music at an elementary school in a working-class section of Philadelphia. Although he enjoyed teaching, he did not regard it as his true vocation. After grading papers and planning for the next day's lessons in the evening, Harris sat at a piano composing operas—book, music, and lyrics.

Harris had completed several operas about world-renowned figures, including Alexander the Great, Moses, and Lincoln. However, he considered his masterpiece the most recent work—*The Trial of Henry Kissinger*, inspired by the Christopher Hitchens book of the same title. He was particularly proud of the finale, as representatives from the various peoples whose lives Kissinger had destroyed, such as the Vietnamese, Cambodians, Chileans, and Timorese, sing "Guilty": first in their native language, then in English, as the curtain descends.

He had submitted the complete score to opera companies in the United States and Europe. The replies were all rejections albeit polite. One day following school dismissal, his colleague Mark noticed Harris sitting in his classroom reading a letter and looking glum.

"Why the long face?" Mark asked.

"Guess."

"Another rejection?"

"That's right."

"From whom?"

"The Milwaukee Opera Company."

"What did they say?"

"The usual—'a brilliant piece but too risky economically for an unknown composer.' I have to face it. I'll probably never see any of my works produced."

"Look," replied Mark, "I have given this some thought. Since part of the problem is your anonymity, you should try to make yourself known. You don't need to be a superstar. What I mean is, if you find a way to establish name recognition, then maybe, by word of mouth, a producer might hear enough about you to take a chance on your work."

"How do I do that?"

"Playout. There are lots of piano bars in the city where you can play your music."

"First of all, I can't sing; and second, I write serious opera, not toe-tapping pop songs."

"Do you have any other talents? Can you act, do magic, dance?"

"No, no, and—dance? Look at me. I'm a klutz even when I walk," said Harris, who was on the heavy side.

"Is there anything you can do as a performer?"

"Well," Harris offered modestly, "some say I can tell a joke."

"Really? Let's hear one."

Harris told his favorite, involving two golfers and a genie. At the punch line, Mark laughed uproariously. "That was a winner! I love the way you used different voices and hand gestures, and your timing was perfect. I think you have a talent there."

Thus, Harris Finkel undertook the long, arduous task of becoming a stand-up comedian. First, he performed at several open mics in the Philadelphia area, which eventually earned him invitations to local and regional competitions. His big break came when he won second prize at the famed Toronto Comedy Festival, which led to appearances on late-night television and headlining at many top comedy clubs,

in both the United States and Canada. The culminating triumph was the selection of Harris to host the Academy Awards ceremony.

Following the show, Harris sat down in his dressing room to remove his makeup. On the table he noticed a letter from The Dallas Opera Company, to which he had recently sent the Kissinger piece. "Another rejection," he thought. Then, with a sigh, he set aside the jar of cleansing cream and opened the envelope. To his amazement, it read as follows:

> Dear Mr. Finkel,
>
> I have reviewed *The Trial of Henry Kissinger*'s score and wish, with your permission, to stage it during our next season. My colleagues and I agree it is a composition of considerable power, originality, and artistic merit. Further, the board of directors foresees no obstacle to its favorable reception and success. Please get in touch with me as soon as possible to discuss the details of what promises to be an exciting and rewarding collaboration.
>
> Sincerely yours,
> David Bellinger
> Artistic Director
> The Dallas Opera Company

Harris immediately telephoned Mark in Philadelphia. "Mark, I have great news! The Dallas Opera Company has agreed to stage the Kissinger piece. I am elated. You were right—get yourself known, and anything can happen."

"Don't you want to talk about the Oscar show? I thought you were fantastic."

"Forget that. This is more important. *Kissinger* will be staged next season. I want you to sit next to me opening night—all expense paid."

"You don't have to do that."

"It's the least I can do. I can't thank you enough. Because of your advice, my dream will come true."

The Trial of Henry Kissinger was scheduled for a two-week run. Opening night was festive. The opera house was vibrant with the formalized sensuality of tuxedos and evening gowns. Harris attended several pre-show cocktail parties, gave interviews, signed autographs, and had his picture taken with wealthy patrons.

When the audience had been seated, Harris entered the concert hall to thunderous applause. He acknowledged the ovation with a wave, then took a VIP chair beside Mark. "Finally," Harris thought, "I can see a work in which I invested so much time and energy."

The conductor took a bow and began the overture. But almost from the first note, something strange happened—people were giggling, and with increasing volume. "What's so funny?" Harris whispered to Mark.

"I was afraid of this," Mark whispered in return.

"Afraid of what?"

"Not now. I'll explain later."

By the end of the first act, gales of laughter were issuing from throughout the hall. Some of the audience even toppled helplessly into the aisles. "Why are they laughing? Why?" Harris wailed.

"Hush—wait till later," Mark insisted.

The sounds of mirth were especially acute during the final scene when Kissinger's victims sang "Guilty! Guilty!" as the curtain fell. Harris immediately retreated with Mark to a room reserved for him.

"What happened? I wrote a serious opera. Why was everyone laughing?" Harris demanded to know.

"It's your brand," Mark answered matter-of-factly.

"My *what?*"

"Your brand. People know you as a comedian, so whatever you do, they'll find amusing. Haven't you noticed that on *Late Night?* You move your hand; people chuckle. You touch your face; people laugh. Unfortunately, comedy is your brand, and nothing you do can change it. If you wrote an opera called *Mengele at Auschwitz,* people would laugh. They'd probably laugh hardest when Jews are led into the gas chambers!"

"My brand? What are you talking about? I am not a box of cereal! I'm a living, breathing creative artist."

"I understand, but as far as the audience is concerned, you are a comedian and nothing else. There's your choice. You can either continue as a comedian or go back to teaching."

Stunned, Harris ranted, "Do you think I *enjoy* being a comedian? Good God, I hate it! It's one of the lowest art forms. Hell—it doesn't even deserve to be an art form. You slip on a banana, and people howl. You call that art? I studied classical music with some of the finest teachers in the country. I can play Bach, Beethoven, Chopin, and look what I'm doing—telling jokes about airline food. And who am I entertaining? A bunch of lazy, ignorant slobs—people I couldn't stand spending two minutes with alone. I once mentioned Liszt to an audience member, and he told me he had a cousin with a *lisp*! Comedy's the last thing I wanted to do. I only took it up so I could get my music produced. That was your advice."

"I know. I just didn't think you'd become this successful."

Mark returned to Philadelphia and met with the school principal. Soon enough, Harris was restored to his former position as an instructor in the music program. However, things had changed. Harris could no longer control his unruly students' behavior, since no matter what he said or did, they laughed.

KEATS

It went like this:

"Drop dead!"

"You first!"

"Good night. Hope it's your last."

Thus would end a typical day in the life of Allen and Josh Seidel. No pair of brothers could have been less compatible. But why should this be so? Was the cause mutual envy or malignancy of another sort?

In his teens, Allen emerged as a star athlete, much admired as the running back of his high school varsity football team. But, unfortunately, this achievement failed to impress his younger brother, who was most contented in solitude, reading English literature—above all, the poetry of John Keats. This difference in personalities was almost too much for Allen to bear. Therefore, he would often go on the offensive, initiating a quarrel in the following manner:

(*Allen taunts.*) "How did I get stuck with a brother like you? You're an embarrassment. All my friends have brothers—even sisters—who like sports. But look what I have—a wimpy faggot who's into Cleats."

(*Josh retorts.*) "One, I'm not a faggot; and two, it's not "Cleats." It's "Keats." So we're different. You love football. I prefer books. I don't see the problem."

(*Allen digs in.*) "It's more than that."

(Josh picks up the bait.) "Like what?"

"You're an old Jew."

(Josh is taken aback.) "How can I be an old Jew? I'm only fifteen years old."

"I mean, you're *like* an old Jew, an old-*fashioned* Jew—just reading and thinking. And after that, more reading and more thinking."

"And what are you?"

(Allen is proud.) "I'm the *new* Jew—the Jew of action, the Jew of muscle. People respect that."

"What people?"

"Everyone—even the goyim."

(Josh, too, is capable of scorn.) "The goyim? They'll kill you a minute after some nutcase president gives the nod. Fine! Move to Israel; work on a kibbutz; and in two weeks, you'll be home complaining of back problems."

(Allen makes sure to get the last word.) "Go to hell—and don't come back!"

****

One Saturday, Allen invited members of the team to his home to watch a college football game. Josh passed them as he headed upstairs to his room. Allen called out for all to hear, "There goes my brilliant brother. Memorizing your Cleats today?"

Josh stopped, turned, and addressed his brother firmly. "The name is Keats. Can't you memorize a simple fact? Now, for your information—and my enlightenment—I'm also reading Mary Shelley's *Frankenstein*. Guess she met you before she wrote it."

"Oh, he got you there," one of the players snickered to Allen as Josh bounded up the steps.

"Oh, sure, he got me. But I'll be making millions in the NFL while he'll be lisping, 'Would you like to supersize that, sir?' Yeah, you better run," Allen yelled to Josh, "before I grab you by your Paul Bunyan."

"The poet you must mean is Lord Byron, Professor!" Josh called down from a safe spot.

At halftime, Allen's teammate Ron Taylor went upstairs to use the bathroom and noticed Josh sitting in his room, reading. "May I come in?" Ron asked courteously.

"Sure," Josh responded with cautious friendliness.

"I'm sorry how your brother treats you."

Josh shrugged. "He's ignorant. What can you say?"

"You like Keats?"

"Yes, he's my favorite writer. Do you know anything about him?"

"To be honest, no. But we did read a poem—'The Hollow Men'—in my English class last month. That's by George Eliot—uh, I mean T. S. Eliot. I think I remember some of it."

"Go ahead. I know it by heart."

"Okay, here goes: 'Between the conception / And the creation / Between the emotion—' Help me."

"'And the response . . .'" Josh supplied.

"'Falls the Shadow . . .' See, I almost got it."

Josh was delighted. "Fantastic!"

"I better go downstairs before your brother gets suspicious. But listen—I have an idea how to get him off your back."

"Tell me."

"Not now. Let me work on it."

The following Friday, there was an announcement over the PA system just before the end of the school day: "There will be a compulsory meeting of the varsity football team in the assembly hall immediately following dismissal." When Allen arrived, he found only the coach. "Where's everyone?" Allen asked.

"Sit down. I wanna show you something," the coach answered. "Okay, gentlemen, come on out."

The entire football team entered from the wings of the stage, with Ron positioned in the middle. Ron stepped forward and declared, "We, the varsity football team of Grover Cleveland High School, now wish to present 'Ode on a Grecian Urn' by John Keats."

Team members stepped forward one by one so that each could perform a couple of lines. For example, left guard Jim Rowan intoned, "Heard melodies are sweet, but those unheard / Are sweeter; therefore, ye soft pipes, play on." Right tackle Ted Miller recited, "And, little town, thy streets for evermore / Will silent be; and not a soul to tell / Why thou art desolate, can e'er return." Ron had the honor of delivering the famous concluding words of the poem: "Beauty is truth, truth beauty,—that is all / Ye know on earth, and all ye need to know."

The coach applauded, then turned to Allen. "As you can see, every individual on this team admires John Keats. Do you have a problem with that?"

"No, sir," Allen stammered, in shock.

"Is there any advice you would like to offer your teammates concerning Keats? They are all here to listen: Now is your opportunity."

"No, sir."

"Now we have another surprise for you. I'd like you to meet our new equipment manager." Josh stepped out to the stage.

"May I assume you know each other?"

"Yes," mumbled Allen, still in a daze.

"How are you acquainted?"

"He's my brother."

"Well, I suggest you be respectful to your brother. After all, you don't want to be issued defective equipment, do you?"

"No, sir."

"Thank you all. Dismissed."

****

Allen never bullied Josh again. He received a partial scholarship to play football for Temple University. Though his competence was notable, his athletic career turned out to be less than stellar. In his sophomore year, now more mature and ashamed for the emotional torture he had inflicted upon his younger brother, Allen chose A Survey of English Literature as an elective. The coursework so piqued his interest that he not only received a bachelor's degree in the field but went on to earn a master's and eventually a doctorate. Indeed, Allen Seidel made a name for himself as one of the world's leading scholars of early medieval English literature.

Josh Seidel was awarded a full scholarship to the University of Pennsylvania and, upon graduation, was hired as equipment manager for the Dallas Cowboys. Popular with the players, he was known for meticulous attention to detail, a strong sense of justice, and a habit rarely observed in a football stadium: reciting antiquated poems from the sidelines.

Twist of the Wrist

Howard himself would be the first to concede that he never achieved much by his own initiative. On the other hand, he also would be the first to acknowledge that he possessed a remarkable gift—or was it a curse?—from God: for he was a human rabbit's foot. In practical terms, this meant that whosoever did a good deed for him, even something as trivial as picking up a pencil, would be rewarded with a life of good luck. As a corollary, whosoever harmed him in any way would experience a life of misfortune.

Evidence abounded: After the star football player in high school mocked Howard, he suffered a career-ending injury. But after a classmate agreed to attend the senior prom with him, her pleasant looks were transfigured to the point of her becoming a noted fashion model. After an uncle deliberately pitched at Howard's head during a softball game, he found himself mysteriously estranged from both his sons. And yet, after another uncle treated Howard to a single hot dog at a carnival, he shocked the entire family by making millions in the stock market.

Now it came to pass that his older brother arrived at Howard's house one day to assist with a computer problem. It happened that the brother's vain but attractive twenty-two-year-old daughter tagged along. As they entered the living room, Howard pointed to a photograph of his new girlfriend, which he had placed with careful affection on a coffee table next to the sofa. "I know she's not beautiful, but we get along," he offered, humbly aware of his niece.

"As long as you're happy, that's what's important," was his brother's mild reply.

While Howard's brother worked on the computer, the niece sat on the sofa, talking and texting to friends from her iPhone and periodically glancing at herself through the phone's camera function to check her

hair and makeup. As soon as the repair was complete, Howard escorted his brother and niece to the front door and said goodbye.

Once back in the living room, Howard was pained to notice that his niece had turned the photograph of his sweetheart around to avoid looking at her. "Poor girl," Howard sighed to himself, "now you will experience a life of hardship and grief on account of a simple twist of the wrist."

PS: There are quite a few "rabbit's foot" people scattered around the world. They may range from a CEO of a large corporation to a street beggar in Bangladesh. Therefore, it is highly advisable that you behave kindly to everyone you meet.

Ex Pede Herculem

No pair of lovers could have seemed more firmly attached than Jon Kopelman and Nicole Shelanski. Both in high school and currently in their twenties, they were nearly inseparable. Indeed, they were so often observed together that friends fondly referred to them as JoNicky and would become worried if either should be spotted without the other. Though they lived apart, they made every effort to meet each day. On the rare occasions when that was not possible, they spoke on the phone every few hours, reporting their whereabouts and activities. Both felt this practice ensured them a level of trust and understanding most couples could never achieve.

One day, during Jon's routine grocery shopping, he noticed a new product on display—a packaged assortment of nuts. On impulse, he bought several bags. Once home, he rushed to open the first bag, and amidst the expected cashews, almonds, hazelnuts, and pecans, he found several of one kind of nut he couldn't identify. Upon trying a sample, he immediately telephoned Nicole.

"Come quick! I need to see you."

"What is it?" Nicole responded. "Are you okay?"

"I'm fine. But come as soon as you can. I've got to show you something."

"Hang in there! I'm on my way," Nicole answered.

As soon as she arrived, Jon held up the mystery nut. "Try this. Tell me if it's not the most delicious nut you've ever eaten."

Nicole popped the nut into her mouth. "Oh, my God! I never tasted such a delicious nut."

"Was I right?"

"You sure were. What kind is it?"

"I don't know. I checked, but the bag didn't list the ingredients. All I know is that each of these bags contains six such nuts. While I was waiting for you, I emptied them all and counted. Let's see: I ate one, and you ate one, so there's four left in the first bag. Here—you take two more, and I'll take two more." Jon handed her two nuts, which she consumed without pause.

"It's wonderful how we share everything," Nicole cooed.

"Isn't it?" Jon beamed. "I love you, Nicole."

"I love you too, Jon."

A few days later, Jon drove Nicole to Atlantic City for a long weekend. On the way, he asked Nicole to reach back and grab an unopened bag of the mixed nuts that were now a symbol of their bond.

"My darling, dig in and give me our special nut," Jon half whispered seductively.

"With all my heart! Here you are."

Jon lingered over the nut with sighs of pleasure. "You know, Nicole? Of course, I like the whole assortment—almonds, cashews, hazelnuts, and pecans—but this one item surpasses the rest by far. To tell you the truth, I could die today knowing I had eaten this nut."

"Hey, what about me?" Nicole pouted. "Don't I count?"

"Of course. I'm just joking. You're my everynut, forever and ever."

After a few more miles, Jon requested his second nut, which Nicole dutifully handed over. Then, after paying a toll, Jon asked for what he knew to be his third and last nut from the pack.

"I'm sorry," Nicole said, "but there's no more left."

"But there has to be another. There are six special nuts in a bag—three for you and three for me. You had your three, right?"

"Yes," Nicole agreed.

"So how come there's no more in the bag? There *has* to be one more for me."

"Jon, I hate to admit this. I may have eaten one of your nuts."

"What?" Jon cried out in amazement. "Are you telling me you ate *four* nuts? You know there are six in a bag. As I just told you, that's three for you and three for me. How could you do this? How could you steal an extra nut?"

"I'm sorry," Nicole stammered. "I guess I wasn't thinking. Those nuts are so good I lost track. Anyway, it's no big deal. I'll buy you your own bag as soon as we arrive."

"That's not the point," Jon ranted. "The point is I specifically said we were each to eat three nuts. The fact that you took four is, to be honest, shocking."

"Jon," she persisted uneasily, "it's not the end of the world. I said I'd buy you another bag. I'll even buy you two or three bags if you'd like. Can we just drop it?"

During their entire time in Atlantic City, Jon said nothing. Whether they were strolling on the boardwalk, sitting on the beach, out for dinner, or seeing a show, Jon remained quiet; nor did he even once hold Nicole's hand as he had always done. And although Nicole attempted by every means to encourage intimacy or at least conversation, he kept a distance, preferring to watch television until falling asleep.

"Jon," Nicole pleaded desperately, "we have only one day left here. Let's make amends and enjoy it. How many times must I say I'm sorry? It was a mistake. I know we agreed to share everything, but this is going too far."

At this, Jon broke his silence. "Do you remember how we met?"

"Not exactly. I just know we met in high school."

"We met in Latin class."

"Oh, yes. I remember."

"I liked learning Latin, and even today, I use some Latin expressions, such as *quid pro quo* or *sine qua non*."

"I'm impressed when you use them. I pretty much forgot everything."

"Well, there was one expression I found especially interesting, though I rarely get a chance to use it."

"What's that?"

"*Ex pede Herculem.*"

"What does it mean?"

"It means 'from the foot of Hercules.'"

"I don't understand."

"It means if you know the size of Hercules's foot, you can estimate how big Hercules is. Or—transposing to our situation—by observing a small behavior, you can get a picture of someone's character."

"So what are you saying?"

"I'm saying that because you took the extra nut, I can see clearly what kind of person you are."

"Which is?"

"You're an extremely selfish person. You think only of yourself, not anyone else. I would almost venture to say your selfishness borders on the psychotic. I recommend you seek professional help."

"From my taking a nut, you conclude I need counseling?"

"Yes."

Nicole protested, "You're insane! We've gone together for eleven years! When have I ever been selfish? Every day when I wake up, my first thought is what I can do for you. And not only then—you're in my thoughts all the time. Even my mother scolds, 'Can't you talk about anything other than your beloved Jon?' I don't know how you can accuse me like that."

"I'm sorry. I must trust what I feel. Let's go home."

Jon was silent on the ride back. He dropped Nicole at her house with a curt nod, returned to his apartment, and composed a letter:

Dear Nicole,

It is with a heavy heart that I must end our relationship. True, these past eleven years were, I long felt, a dream joyfully fulfilled. There are many things I will miss about you—your cheerful smile; your spontaneous laugh; your exquisite fashion sense; and your talent for engaging conversation, which enlivens any gathering you join. And yet, there has come to my attention a negative that outweighs all of those positive attributes: that is, your incurably selfish nature. Yes, I understand how taking the nut may seem inconsequential and even ridiculous to you. However, to me, this incident is of the utmost gravity. For it provided a clear view of the person behind the charming mask—a woman of rampant, rapacious, and rabid self-centeredness.

The truth is, I had intended to propose marriage during our trip to Atlantic City. I kept the ring close, in my pocket, and was waiting for an opportunity to speak. However, it was not to be. Though I am not an especially observant Jew, I nevertheless see the hand of God in all things, and I believe it was He who intervened at the last moment and saved me from a lifetime of misery. As stated in the book of Samuel, "People judge by outward appearances, but the Lord looks at the heart." God looked into your heart, found it wanting, and warned me thus. Nevertheless, I wish you well, whatever path you follow. Please give my best to your mother.

With deep regret and sincere regard, Jon

****

Years passed. One day, while relaxing at his favorite twenty-four-hour diner, Jon noticed a man and woman sitting across from each other at the other end of the room. Though the woman's back was turned to him, he was almost sure it was Nicole, whom he had not seen in nearly a decade. He stood and approached their table.

"Nicole, is that you?" Jon asked, peering at her cautiously.

"Oh, my God! Jon! I can't believe it! How *are* you?"

"Good. I'm an accountant—and single. Mom's still thriving at ninety-five, and I hope I take after her."

"That's wonderful. Please give her my best."

"I will. And how are *you?*"

"Doing great. This is my husband, Alex—a doctor, of course."

"Nice to meet you," Jon said as they shook hands.

"And this is Jon," continued Nicole.

"How do you know each other?" Alex asked Nicole.

"I'm sure you remember. I've told you about Jon. We went together for almost twelve years."

Alex did indeed remember the story and forgot his habitual tact. "Oh—is this the guy with the nut?"

"That's me," Jon gulped, unable to conceal his embarrassment. "Nicole, I am so sorry about what happened and that crazy letter I wrote to you. I'm mortified every time I recall it. I can't believe how I could break up with such a fine person—and over a nut. I was out of my mind."

"No problem. It all worked out. I married a wonderful man, have two amazing kids, a beautiful home, and even a head-turning car. Sit down. Let me show you some pictures."

Jon sat next to Nicole while she proudly showed photos of well-pampered children, a spacious, spotless house, a dazzling car, and family vacations in exotic overseas islands. Jon's response was held tightly within, but Nicole smiled with satisfaction. "Well, if you'll excuse me, I need to use the restroom. Why don't the two of you have a chat? I'll be back soon."

"Yeah, keep me company," Alex added.

As soon as Nicole was out of view, Alex leaned urgently into Jon. "Look, I have only a few minutes, so I must talk fast. Let me tell you something. You dodged a bullet. You could not believe what a selfish woman Nicole is. All she thinks about is herself. Day and night, it's I, I, I; ME, ME, ME. I'd be out of this marriage

in a second, except I'd be killed financially. So take it from me: you have nothing to feel sorry about. You did the right thing. I only wish I had done the same."

Nicole returned to the table, and after a brief exchange of pleasantries, they all said goodbye. It was one o'clock in the afternoon when Jon began eating, and he sat there until the following morning.

Stouthearted Man of the Year

"**H**oney, I'm home!" Sam Gelsher announced with excitement as he strode proudly across the front-door threshold. "I have great news!"

Sam's wife, Beth, did not trouble herself to turn around and face him. "Huh?" she mumbled indifferently, her eyes remaining glued to the television.

"Please turn off the TV. You gotta hear this."

Beth did not conceal her annoyance. "Can't it wait? This is my favorite program. I look forward to it all week."

"Beth, please," Sam implored, though his exuberance was waning.

"Okay, okay," she sighed. "I'll put down the volume. Now, what's so important?"

Sam attempted to recover his enthusiasm. "I'm getting an award."

"From who?"

"The lodge."

"The *lodge*?"

"Yes."

"What kind of award? The Takes a Thousand Years to Make Up Your Mind certificate of merit?"

Sam chose to ignore the sarcasm, though it pained him as usual. "No. I've been named Stouthearted Man of the Year."

At this, Beth was shocked enough to turn and face Sam. "Stouthearted Man of the Year? What's that mean?"

"Stouthearted. It means brave, dauntless, and determined."

"Who?"

"Me."

"The lodge thinks you're brave?"

"Yes."

"And what else?"

"Dauntless and determined."

"What's that mean?"

"Dauntless. It means fearless."

"The lodge thinks you're fearless?"

"That's right."

"And what's that last word?"

"Determined."

"The lodge thinks you're dauntless and determined?"

"Yes."

"Hold on." She lowered the television volume another notch. "Am I hearing this right? You're getting an award for brave, fearless, and determined?"

"Yes. Lenny called me this afternoon and told me the executive board chose me for the award. It will be presented at next month's charity auction."

"Are you sure they got the right person? I mean brave? When have you been brave? What—taking the trash out during a thunderstorm? That's brave? Are you sure they just don't mean *stout*? I mean, let's face it—a diet wouldn't hurt."

Though nearly deflated, Sam pressed on. "Well, I'm simply reporting what I heard. Like I said, it will be presented at next month's charity auction." "I wouldn't miss it for the world," Beth offered before raising the volume on the television.

During the weeks leading up to the event, Beth couldn't resist chatting with friends about the award—for example, when she called Pearl, her bosom buddy. "Pearl, are you sitting?"

"Yes. Why?"

"I wouldn't want you to keel over after hearing what I'm about to tell you."

"Tell me what?"

"It's Sam. He's getting an award."

"An award? What kind of award?"

"Stouthearted . . . Man . . . of the Year," Beth enunciated slowly.

"Excuse me, say that again."

"Stouthearted Man of the Year."

"Stouthearted Man of the Year? What's that mean?"

"Stouthearted. It means brave and determined."

"Who?"

"Sam."

"Sam's brave and determined?"

"Yes."

"Who thinks that?"

"The lodge."

"The lodge thinks Sam's brave and determined?"

"Yes."

"Sam. Sam Gelsher."

"That's right. Our Sam. He's getting the award at next month's charity auction."

"I wouldn't miss it for the world."

"That's exactly what I said."

"Beth, forgive me. I'm about to have a laughing fit."

"You? I haven't stopped laughing for weeks. Talk to you later."

The evening of the charity event arrived. Sam and Beth entered the auditorium and took their seats as the lodge president, Jack Munstein, stepped forward.

"Ladies and gentlemen, thank you very much for attending our annual fundraising meeting. We have several fantastic items up for auction this evening, so please open your hearts and your wallets, and let's make this event an evening to remember.

"But before we begin the auction, we would like to honor our Stouthearted Man of the Year. For those new members who are not acquainted with our ceremonies, let me explain. Each year we present an award named after the song 'Stout-Hearted Men,' written in 1928 by Oscar Hammerstein and Sigmund Romberg. It includes these lyrics:

> Give me some men who are stout-hearted men

Who will fight for the right they adore
Start me with ten who are stout-hearted men
And I'll soon give you ten thousand more.

"In other words, a stouthearted man is one who is brave and determined. To be honest, we did not intend to give the award this year, as we had not identified a member who truly exemplified those qualities. However, I recently received a letter from the president of JWV—the Jewish War Veterans. I will read it to you:

Dear Mr. Munstein,

It has come to our attention that one of your members—Sergeant Samuel P. Gelsher—demonstrated exceptional valor during the Vietnam War. In 1968, the Vietnamese coastal city of Da Nang was attacked by two heavily armed North Vietnamese battalions. During the onslaught, Sergeant Gelsher, then serving in the Eighty-Second Airborne, was informed that many civilians were trapped inside a building. Under his command, soldiers stormed the building, drove out the enemy, and rescued twenty-three civilians. For this brave deed, Sergeant Gelsher received the Silver Star, awarded to those who display—and I quote—'gallantry in action against an enemy of the United States.' We trust that you and the entire lodge membership will feel honored and blessed to have a man of such merit in your midst.

Respectfully,
Lawrence Schulman
National Commander of the Jewish War Veterans of the United States."

President Munstein looked up, beaming, and concluded, "Will Sergeant Samuel P. Gelsher please rise and accept a token of our esteem."

Sam rose, made his way to the podium in somewhat of a daze, and received an engraved trophy to joyous cheers and thunderous applause. When he returned to his seat, Beth stammered, "Oh, Sam! You never told me. Why didn't you say anything? I feel terrible making fun of you like that. Sam, are you listening? Sam. Sam!"

Sam thought he heard a voice but was too engaged in battle to see who it was.

THE READING OF THE WILL

Could any two siblings have outdone the Weisman boys in violating the principle of brotherly love? Through childhood, adolescence, the teen years, and adulthood, they hated each other with a ferocity usually assigned to warring primitive tribesmen rather than to educated, acceptably cultured professionals such as Simon, a medical doctor, and Eric, a professor of ancient history. Though they studiously avoided coming to fisticuffs, each grasped every opportunity to hurl insulting remarks regarding the other's personality, physical appearance, domestic arrangements, and vocation.

An objective observer might wonder how such implacable antagonists had the self-discipline to simulate heartfelt affection towards each other in their parents' presence—which Simon and Eric did so as not to cause alarm by revealing their deep-seated animosity. Indeed, family acquaintances had rarely observed two brothers who appeared to love each other so profoundly. Often they would confide to the well-meaning, yet clueless, elder Weismans, "I wish my children would get along as well as Simon and Eric. You are truly blessed."

The ruse continued after their father had passed, again so as not to upset their mother, who felt her most outstanding achievement had been to produce such compatible sons. "Promise me that after I'm gone, you will continue to take care of each other. Remember, nothing is more important than family," she would instruct them.

"We will, Mom. You don't have to worry," Eric would reassure her playfully. "History will record our relationship as a classic: it has stood the test of time."

"I'm so happy to hear that," she would sigh in relief. "Of course, I hope to live many more years, but at least I can die in peace knowing what you have just said."

"Mother," Simon would add with mock solemnity, "I swear by my physician's oath to extend your life by ensuring the health of our family bond."

Soon after their mother's death, Simon and Eric found themselves at close quarters in the office of Harold Rosen, a longtime family friend and the executor of her will. The two sat across from Rosen, making every effort to avoid eye contact. "Well, gentlemen," Rosen began, "I am about to read the last will and testament of your mother. Please listen carefully: 'I, Sylvia Weisman, being of sound mind and memory do hereby declare this to be my last will and testament.'"

"Mr. Rosen," Simon interrupted, "with all respect, I believe the reading of the will is a relic of the past. Am I right?"

"That's true," Rosen conceded. "I just thought you would appreciate the formality. For some families, it brings a kind of closure."

"We understand," Eric pursued evenly, "but Simon and I have read the document several times and agree not to contest any part of it. If you could please show us where to sign, we can go on our way."

"Well, if that's what you want, so be it." Rosen placed various papers on his desk, provided pens, and indicated the spaces for signature.

Next, without further ceremony, Eric handed Rosen a check. "This is your fee and a little extra. Thank you for all your work and for being so kind to our parents through the years."

"It's been my pleasure," Rosen smiled with satisfaction. "You know what I enjoyed most about your family? I noticed the remarkable companionship between the two of you. I've never known two brothers with such love for each other."

"Mr. Rosen," Simon responded flatly, "it was just an act. The truth is, Eric and I despise each other. We've loathed each other since we were kids. We simply didn't want our parents to become disillusioned. Believe me, when not with our parents, we couldn't stand the sight of each other."

"Is that—is that true?" Rosen stammered, incredulous.

"Yes, it's true," Eric affirmed. "I've been longing for this day because once we leave this room, I don't have to set eyes on this worthless slimeball ever again!"

"Slimeball?" Simon sneered. "You're so low on the evolutionary scale, slime would be an improvement!"

"Your wife's slime!" Eric countered.

"So's yours!"

"Boys—gentlemen!" Rosen anxiously interjected. "Perhaps it would be best if you could take this outside. I have other clients coming in shortly."

Simon and Eric grabbed their jackets, marched out of the office, and took an elevator to street level. "Well, this is it," Simon declared as he zipped up his jacket.

"This is it," Eric promptly agreed.

"Just remember," Simon warned. "Don't ever call me, don't text me—nothing, nada. If you happen to see me on the street or, God forbid, in a restaurant, act like you don't know me, understand?"

"Same here and double," Eric one-upped him.

"Good—and goodbye," Simon snarled.

"Goodbye!"

As Simon walked away, Eric called out, "Simon!"

Simon turned. "What?"

"Hungry?"

"I could eat. Know somewhere?"

"Follow me."

Doors

Though Andy Gottlieb functioned normally in most respects, he was chronically tardy because of a debilitating behavior—the habit of confirming and reconfirming that he had locked the door when leaving his house. In a typical episode, he would stand outside pushing and pulling the front door for nearly fifteen minutes, then walk to his car, then return to check for another fifteen minutes. Many were the times he would drive almost ten miles, turn around, speed home, and check again.

Andy's inability to report to work on time cost him numerous warnings and threats of termination. His problem created unfortunate situations in his personal life as well. He was late for important social events, for example, when he rushed to his brother's home for the Passover seder, only to find the service over and the meal eaten, and when he missed being called to the Torah at his nephew's bar mitzvah. He even arrived at his mother's surprise eightieth birthday party just as the guests were leaving, though he had arranged the entire event!

Andy's girlfriend, the long-suffering Miriam, continually urged him to seek professional help. "I don't need help," he insisted. "It's perfectly normal. Haven't you heard the expression 'fashionably late'?"

"Fashionably late means fifteen minutes—or at most, a half hour. It doesn't mean two weeks!" Miriam would respond, hoping the hyperbole would shake him into action. But this tactic was no more successful than any other.

The turning point was Andy's failure to appear at a dinner honoring Miriam as "Employee of the Year." After this mortification, she issued an ultimatum: "Either you get help, or I'm leaving you." Shocked into

recognizing that she was more precious than his irrational self-indulgence, he searched for a therapist specializing in obsessive-compulsive behavior.

Dr. Frederick Schuler was known for his interest in the connection between specific linguistic structures and the psyche, particularly what he called "the movement of the mind through metaphor." Thus, when probing a patient afflicted with a fixation, he would sift the speech accidents for clues. "Feeling driven to constantly check the front door may be related to a deep psychological need for safety," Schuler suggested to Andy. "First, have you ever been a victim of a robbery or break-in?"

"No, never," Andy responded firmly.

"How about your childhood? Did you feel safe growing up?"

"Very much. My parents provided a warm, supportive, and loving environment."

"Any problems with siblings?"

"Not at all. My older brothers were always there to defend or help me if I had any difficulty."

"How about friends?" the doctor pursued. "Other than Miriam, do you have many close friends?"

"I'm afraid not," Andy admitted.

"Why is that?"

Andy explained, rather testily, "I guess you could say I don't suffer fools lightly. I tend to have a short fuse, so, as a result, I often close doors."

Schuler's interest was piqued. He leaned forward. "What did you say?"

"I said I have a short fuse."

"No, you said something else."

"I don't suffer fools?"

"Not that. Recall the last thing you said."

"Oh, I close doors."

"That's it! There's your answer. You need to reopen those doors!"

"What do you mean?"

"I believe that your obsession with checking the front door is a symbolic enactment of your ending relationships with friends. I'm thus certain that the more you reestablish your relationships—the more you open up—the less you will feel the need to check and recheck your door."

"Doctor, thank you. Let me go. I have much work to do."

Thus, Andy diligently set about restoring friendships with all those he had turned his back on, and he found that his simple humility was accepted graciously. As the doctor had predicted, Andy's need to check the front door decreased accordingly in stages. The fifteen-minute ritual dwindled—first to twelve, then ten, eight, five, and finally an acceptable three.

Grateful and delighted, Andy invited his formerly shunned friends to dinner at a high-end restaurant. As he and the now-exuberant Miriam conversed with the guests, he received a call from the police informing him that his house had been burglarized. It appeared that before leaving, Andy had forgotten to check the front door.

THE CHECK

Over the months, Avi had been taking his eighty-five-year-old mother out for dinner two or three times a week. Although he could have performed any number of kindnesses during the year since his father had passed away, he had decided it was most meaningful to spend plenty of one-on-one time with his mother, who, he knew, would be grieving for the long term. However, despite Avi's wish to relieve her sorrow, her behavior increasingly rankled him. For all the occasions they went out to eat, his mother did not pick up the check. It was not that he couldn't afford it—in fact, the expense was no burden. But it was the principle that mattered: He didn't think it fair that he should continually pay while his mother didn't
even offer to take a turn.

One evening, when he could no longer contain his resentment, Avi leaned forward earnestly as the check arrived. "Mom, there's something I need to discuss with you."

"Go ahead, dear," his mother replied pleasantly, patting her lips delicately with her napkin.

"We've been going out to dinner frequently since Daddy died, and never did you pay the check or even offer to pay."

Her expression hardened on the instant. "What do you mean?"

"Exactly what I said: It wouldn't hurt if you picked up the check once in a while, or at least offered."

Incredulous, she drew herself back. "*I* should pick up the check?"

"I don't mean all the time. I mean sometimes."

"You can't afford it?"

"I can afford it."

"So," she reasoned, "if you can afford it, why do I have to pick up the check?"

"You don't *have* to pick up the check, but it would be a nice gesture. I just don't think it's fair I pay every time we go out—that's all."

"So you want me to pay?"

"Sometimes. Not every time!" Avi nearly shouted.

"There's no need to shout," she admonished him.

"I'm not shouting," he retorted, struggling to control his volume.

"Yes, you are," his mother insisted. "Maybe you can't hear yourself, but I can."

"I'm sorry," he conceded, although annoyed at his mother's tactic of deflection.

"That's better," she nodded with satisfaction. "So, what were you saying?"

"Once again, I'm saying it wouldn't hurt if you paid now and then. That's all. I'm not telling you to pay every time. That would be ridiculous."

His mother tried a new angle of attack. "Why are you sweating?"

"I'm not sweating."

"Yes, you are. I see beads of sweat on your forehead. Here, take a napkin." Avi accepted the napkin and wiped his face.

"Please, Mom, you understand what I'm trying to say?"

"Sure—you want to make me pay."

"Just sometimes, not all the time, and no one's *making* you!" he exclaimed, exasperated.

She shook her head. "There you go. You're shouting again."

"I'm not shouting!" Avi shouted.

"And how does your brother feel about this?"

"Same as me."

"Wonderful. I have two sons ganging up on me."

"We're not ganging up on you!"

"My God, keep your voice down. Don't you know how to behave in a restaurant? People are starting to stare. And wipe your face. Are you coming down with something?"

"I'm perfectly fine."

"You don't look fine. When we get home, let me give you my doctor's phone number."

"I don't need your doctor's number. I have my own doctor. Do you understand what I'm trying to say?"

"Of course I understand. You're asking an eighty-five-year-old widow, in failing health—"

"Failing health? I was there at your last checkup, remember? The doctor said he never saw a woman your age in such good health."

"Who can barely walk—"

"You can walk! You could compete in a marathon."

"Expecting a common pensioner—"

"Pensioner? Daddy practically left you a millionaire!"

". . . to pick up the tab for her own fully grown son."

"You know what? Forget it. I'm sorry I brought it up. No problem—I'll pay. Are you ready? Let's go."

Avi drove his mother to her house, gave her the customary peck on the cheek, and noted how vigorously she strode to the front door. Once inside, she immediately telephoned her best friend, who was facing a similar situation with *her* son.

"It's simple. All you have to do is tell him you're in bad health, can't walk, and are heading for the poorhouse. Believe me—he'll give up."

But Is He Jewish?

Every Saturday, I visit my venerable mother to take her to lunch. On a recent occasion, as she greeted me at the door, I could hear water running upstairs. A quick inspection revealed that the water was circulating endlessly in her toilet. After failing to fix it, I used my iPhone to locate a plumber based nearby. The plumber said he'd be there within an hour, which led to the following conversation with Mom.

Me: I called a plumber. Good news—he'll be here shortly.

Mom: Is he Jewish?

Me: What?

Mom: Is he Jewish? Did you ask if he's Jewish?

Me: What are you talking about?

Mom: I'd like to know if he's Jewish, that's all.

Me: Are you out of your mind? You think I'm gonna ask if he's Jewish? What does that have to do with anything? He's a plumber. He's coming to fix the toilet. Who cares if he's Jewish?

Mom: What am I asking? I'd just like to know if he's Jewish. That's all. What's so bad?

Me: It doesn't matter if he's Jewish or not. Plumbers are busy, especially on a Saturday. You should be grateful he's coming at all. Such a thing—"Is he Jewish?"

Mom: What's his name?

Me: Len.

Mom: Len? Len *what?*

Me: That's the name of his company—Len's Plumbing.

Mom: So you couldn't ask?

Me: Ask what?

Mom: His last name. That way I'd know if he's Jewish.

Me: No, I didn't ask his last name.

Mom: What's so hard? He answers the phone: "Len's Plumbing. Can I help you?" You say, "Is this Len?" He says, "Yes." Then you say, "Len *what?*" Then he tells you his last name. Problem solved.

Me: There's no problem! Enough with the Jewish. He's coming to fix the toilet, not daven[7]!

Mom: Don't get so excited. Why you have to get so excited? I'm only talking. What, I'm not allowed to talk?

I look out the window and see a truck pulling up.

Me: I think he's here. Mom, do me a favor. Wait in the kitchen. I'll call you when he's done.

Mom: I can't meet him?

Me: So you can ask if he's Jewish? I'm not taking any chances. Please, wait in the kitchen.

Mom: I'm not going anywhere.

Me: Please!

Mom: (*pause; dramatic sigh*) All right.

---

7.   **Daven:** Recite prayers.

Mom withdraws to the kitchen as Len enters the house. I lead him upstairs, show him the toilet, and return downstairs to wait in the living room. After about fifteen minutes, Len comes down.

Len: All done! Just needed a new flapper.

Me: I figured that. How much do I owe you?

Len: Make it fifty—but could you do me a favor? It's the Jewish Sabbath, and I'm not permitted to touch money or even handle a check. To be honest, I shouldn't even be working today, but we're short-staffed. Anyway, I'll come back tomorrow and pick up the payment, if you don't mind.

Me: Mom! Mom!

Elizabeth Levine: The Jewish Shirley Temple

Though falling tragically short of the renown and iconic stature of Shirley Temple, Elizabeth Levine merits an honorable mention for her brief but successful career as a winsome child actress who starred in such films as *I Love Abe Fertig* and *Sol Green Rides Again*. She was particularly admired for *Who Knew?*—the story of Seymour Litz, a financial advisor who, whether through his own machinations or the workings of fate, miraculously lost all his clients' money *before* the crash of 1929. In this movie, Elizabeth uttered her most memorable line: "It's all right, Seymour. Let's go across the street and get borscht." An alert agent later advised Elizabeth to choose *Get Borscht* for the title of her autobiography.

Like Shirley Temple, Elizabeth retired from show business in 1950 at the age of twenty-two. However, unlike Temple, who developed into a mature, handsome woman, Elizabeth was saddled with an affliction that would haunt her for the remainder of her life—perpetual, immutable cuteness. As a result, no matter how fiercely she attempted to persuade her fans otherwise, she was forever viewed as that little girl who tap-danced with Abe Fertig, comforted Sol Green as he lay dying after a gunfight, or led Seymour Litz through the hollow corridors of Wall Street. Nor did it matter that, by the age of forty-five, she had been married and divorced three times: the public refused to see her as anything other than America's childhood sweetheart.

Thus stymied and stunted, Elizabeth was consumed by an implacable resentment of the wholesome Shirley. So while the adult Shirley Temple sat on the boards of the Walt Disney Company, Del Monte Foods, and the National Wildlife Federation, and in the mid-1970s served as the United States ambassador to Ghana, Elizabeth Levine devoted most of her time, energy, and money to plastic surgery, hoping to extinguish those features that ensured her image as cute. And although there was some minor progress, ultimately doctors were forced to admit they could not achieve the fundamentally impossible.

Elizabeth's final years were even further darkened by the custom of referring to the elderly as cute. For example, one day, when an acquaintance casually remarked, "You look so cute in your new hat," it took three brawny young men to restrain her as she raved, "You say that again, I'll kill ya. I swear I'll kill ya!"

Elizabeth Levine breathed her last in a California nursing home at the venerable age of ninety-two. Whereas the entire world had briefly paused its quarrels to mourn Shirley Temple's passing in 2014, hardly anyone was stirred by Elizabeth's demise. Fortunately, she was unable to hear the rabbi who intoned, while gazing down upon the open casket, "Even in death, as you can see, Elizabeth retained her eternal cuteness: truly a gift from the Almighty."

I Died for the Jews

Though most of David Gendelman's friends were Jewish, he had one Catholic friend, Gladys, whom he had met while waiting in line at a coffee shop. Though never physically intimate, they developed a close emotional bond and a mutual understanding so strong that they often communicated without words.

Besides sharing experiences such as travel, Broadway shows, and exotic restaurants, they shared each other's religious culture. For instance, Gladys took part in a Passover seder with David's family, attended both a bat and a bar mitzvah, and was present at a shiva for David's grandfather. Likewise, David experienced a christening, numerous Catholic weddings, and Midnight Mass on Christmas Eve.

Although David's friends and family were cordial and pleasant towards Gladys, he was impressed by the more profound warmth and kindliness of those in Gladys's inner circle towards him. Further, he observed that attendees at Catholic events typically asked him about himself, demonstrated sincere concern for his aging mother, and spoke humbly about themselves. This, David perceived, was in contrast to Jewish functions, where participants generally spoke unhesitatingly about themselves, announced their latest material acquisitions, and bragged about their children as if they were poised to win the Nobel Prize at six years old!

The difference was so stark in David's mind that he made an appointment to meet the monsignor of Gladys's church. Ushered into an ornate office, David cautiously inquired as follows: "Monsignor, please help me understand something that has been weighing on my mind. As you know, Gladys and I are quite close, and so I have met many of her friends and family and have attended many Catholic events. And on each occasion, I am touched by the depth and quality of the kindness that flows out towards me. You see, though I don't wish to speak ill of my Jewish heritage, the contrast could not be more striking. I'm not suggesting that Jewish people—my people—are rude. No, not at all: my friends and family have been

lovely towards Gladys. And yet, I sense that something is missing in one community that abounds in the other. May I ask, Monsignor, how two peoples could be so different?"

"The answer is simple," the monsignor responded. "Christ died for our sins."

David was startled. "I'm confused. Could you please explain?"

"Jesus Christ, our Lord and Savior, died for our sins. Therefore we, as Catholics, are obliged to live as Jesus would want us to live: that is, a life of love, compassion, understanding, and humility—those qualities Jesus exhibited throughout *his* life. Thus when you encounter a Catholic, he or she is trying to imitate those same qualities I just described. Do you understand?"

"Yes, Monsignor, and thank you for speaking with me." Returning home, David thought long and hard about what the monsignor had said and thus came to a conclusion: *He* would die for the Jews. The following day he met his best friend, Louis, at their favorite Jewish delicatessen.

"Lou," David began, "I need to tell you something."

"What?" Lou asked while munching on a corned beef special.

"I've come to a conclusion."

"What's that?"

"I'm going to die for the Jews."

"What?"

"That's right. I'm going to die for the Jews."

"What the hell you talking about—'die for the Jews'?"

"That's what I've decided. I spoke to the monsignor at Gladys's church, and he explained that Catholics are friendly because Jesus died for them. Therefore, I'm going to die for the Jews. Come on. I've told you many times how friendly Catholics are compared to Jews. Now I know why. The monsignor explained they're friendly because they're trying to imitate the life of Jesus. You see?"

"So because some goy asked you about your car brakes, you're gonna die for the Jews?"

"It's more than car brakes, but that's right. Maybe my death will help change Jewish behavior."

"You know, I thought changing your middle name was nuts, but this takes the cake. No Jew is going to change his behavior because you died. I certainly won't."

"I know that. But think about it. How many people witnessed Jesus's crucifixion—thirty, maybe forty? And today, there are over two and a half billion Christians in the world. So I'm not dying for today's Jews. I'm dying for future generations. Perhaps a thousand years from now Jews will say, 'David Gendelman died for the Jews.'"

"How do you intend to do this?"

"I expect to die a natural death, but I've already instructed the funeral home to engrave 'I died for the Jews' on my stone. If anyone asks, you can tell them."

"Wait, I have a better idea. Why not stage a real crucifixion? Abe Goldstein's a carpenter. He can build a cross. Jack Skolnick owns a hardware store. He can supply the hammer and nails, and we can get Shirley from the Sisterhood to play Jesus's mother."

"Always with the jokes."

****

Two years later, David passed away. A year after that, the ceremonial unveiling revealed the inscription on his headstone:

DAVID GENDELMAN
APRIL 18, 1947–MARCH 3, 2008
I DIED FOR THE JEWS

Needless to say, many were surprised. "Lou," a cousin asked, "you were his best friend. Why did he put 'I died for the Jews' on the stone?"

Too embarrassed to explain, Lou responded, "How the hell should I know? What do you expect from a guy who legally changes his middle name?"

After the service, all attendees went to David's favorite Jewish delicatessen. Once seated, they spoke mainly of themselves, trumpeted their latest consumer acquisitions, and, of course, boasted about their remarkable children.

Mensch

After completing his shift at Temple University Hospital, Doctor Solomon Weinberg had just reached his car when a young man named Marcos approached him.

"Hey, mister, think you can help me?" the man asked.

"What's the problem?"

"It's an emergency. I just got a call from my ex. My daughter got hit by a car. She's in the hospital, and I don't have enough money to get there."

"Which hospital?"

"Cooper, in Camden. I was hoping maybe you could help me out."

"Get in the car. I'll take you. I'm a doctor. I know the people at Cooper."

"That's okay. I can take a train. Drops me right off. Just need a few bucks."

"Get in. It's no trouble. A train takes too long."

"I don't mind. Just need some money. Can you help me out?"

"How much you need?"

"Fifty. Sixty be better."

Solomon reached into his pocket, took out some bills, and counted. "Here's sixty, and here's my card. Give me a call. I wanna know how your daughter's doing," he said as he handed Marcos the money and card.

"Thanks."

"Call me. I mean it."

"I will."

Solomon entered his car and drove off as Marcos stood and watched.

Two days later, Solomon was opening his car door when he spotted Marcos across the street, talking to his Uncle Harold. He beckoned to Marcos to come over.

"What does he want?" Harold asked.

"I don't know."

"Come here!" Solomon called.

"Go see what he wants," Harold said.

Marcos approached Solomon. "How's your daughter? I was waiting for your call."

"My what?" Marcos asked.

"Your daughter. You told me your daughter got hit by a car."

"I don't have no daughter. What're you talkin' about?"

"You told me your daughter got hit by a car. I gave you money to get to Cooper." Solomon paused. "Oh, I get it," Solomon said, realizing he'd been tricked. "That's okay. No problem."

"Oh, yeah. You're the doctor. My daughter. She's doing great. Nothing to worry about."

"Glad to hear it," Solomon answered as he was about to step into the car.

"No. She's doing great. Hardly a scratch."

Solomon stopped and looked at Marcos. "What's your name?" Solomon asked.

"Marcos."

Solomon shut the door and walked to where Marcos was standing. "Marcos, stop lying. I get it. You told me a story, I fell for it, and you got a few bucks, right?"

"Yeah," Marcos answered reluctantly.

"Listen. I'm Jewish, and there's a word Jews use, but anyone can use it. The word is *mensch*. Did you ever hear that word?"

"No."

"It means a man. But more than that, it means a man of honor and integrity. I'm telling you this because you're young. You didn't have to lie to me. You tell me you need money; maybe I give it to you or maybe I won't, but at least you keep your self-respect. Do you understand what I'm saying?"

"Yeah."

"There, you learned something. I have to go. I'm sure I'll see you around. Bye." Solomon entered his car and drove off while Marcos returned to his uncle.

"What he want?"

"Ah, got caught in a lie. I told him the daughter story, and I forgot about it."

"So you feel bad?"

"Little."

"So what? How much you get?"

"Sixty."

"Sixty bucks for a few minutes' work. Nothing to feel bad about. And how many times do I have to tell you? Stop with your damn stories. You don't need a story. Show your gun, take his stuff, and leave. That's it. If he gives you any trouble, you cap the bitch. Get it?"

"Uncle Harold, I've told you many times. I don't have a gun, I don't need a gun, and I don't want a gun."

"How you expect to be a thug without a gun? Everyone needs a gun. Next time I see him, I'll show you how it's done. And I don't need no dumb-ass story either. Now get your sorry ass home."

Marcos returned home, turned on his computer, and looked up the word *mensch*. There he found what Solomon had said: "a person of integrity and honor." He also read "someone you can count on," "someone you can trust," "a stand-up guy," "someone with a sense of what is right."

"Yes," Marcos thought, "from this point on, I will be a mensch."

The following day Marcos and his uncle were in conversation when they spotted Solomon walking towards his car. "Hey, ain't that your friend?" Harold asked.

"No," Marcos answered, remembering what his uncle intended to do.

"Yes, it is. Now watch how a pro does it. Follow me." Harold strode towards Solomon with Marcos in tow.

"Be cool, man. Come on, leave him alone. You need money? I got money. How much you need?" Marcos said anxiously.

"I don't need your damn money. I'm gonna show you how it's done. Quick and easy. Now shut up and watch." Harold went right up to Solomon and pulled a gun from his back pocket. "You know the drill. Hand it over. Everything—money, wallet, that watch. Hurry up!"

"Leave him alone!" Marcos demanded. "I'm serious. Leave him alone!"

"Yeah, whatcha gonna do about it?"

Marcos planted himself between the two men.

"Get out of the way!" Harold exclaimed.

"No. Leave him alone."

"I said move!

"No!"

Harold stared at Marcos, then put the gun back into his pocket. "I'll be talking to you later," Harold growled as he turned and left.

"Thank you," Solomon said as they watched Harold retreat.

"Guess that makes me a mensch," said Marcos. "Right? I'm a mensch."

"Yes, you are. A real mensch."

My Dinner with Herb

Every Wednesday for the past two years, I've been meeting my friend, Herb Lipchitz, for dinner at Midway Diner. This evening Herb selects the chopped sirloin platter while I settle on the chicken salad club sandwich. As soon as we finish ordering, Herb excuses himself to use the men's room. Unfortunately, he's still absent when the food arrives. By the time Herb returns to the table, I'm annoyed, which prompts
the following exchange:

Me: What were you doing so long?

Herb: I saw a sign in the men's room—Employees Must Wash Hands—so I waited for an employee to wash my hands. But no one came.

Me: What?

Herb: *(explaining patiently)* The sign in the restroom said "Employees must wash hands," so I waited for someone to come in and wash my hands. Guess they were too busy working out front.

Me: It's for employees to wash *their* hands, not yours!

Herb: Are you sure?

Me: Yes!

Herb: Maybe the waitress can do it.

Me: Just eat.

Herb: Say—I watched a documentary about World War II last night. You know, if I were alive then, I would have killed Hitler.

Me: Of course. The combined might of the United States, England, and Russia couldn't do it, but Herb Lipchitz—of Cherry Hill, New Jersey—no problem.

Herb: That's right. Next, I watched a documentary about space aliens. Did you know space aliens built the pyramids?

Me: What?

Herb: Space aliens built the pyramids. That's what the documentary said.

Me: And you believe it?

Herb: Why not? Better space aliens do it. Some of those stones weighed as much as three tons. What, people should do that? They were lucky they could find aliens to do it.

Me: I suppose they built the Sphinx too.

Herb: Of course. They were in the neighborhood. Why stop with the pyramids? That would have made no sense.

Me: You know, Herb, I may disagree with what you say, but I will fight to the death for your right to say it.

Herb: Really? You'd fight to the death?

Me: Absolutely—*your* death.

Herb: Ha-ha. So, how'd you do in the Kentucky Derby?

Me: I lost.

Herb: You should have picked Medina Spirit. He won.

Me: So what you're saying is, I should have put my money on the winning horse?

Herb: That's right.

Me: I'll remember that. "Put my money on the winning horse." Thanks. I'll have that laminated.

Herb: Don't mention it.

Me: How's your love life?

Herb: Zero.

Me: Look, I keep telling you. The problem's your name. No woman wants to go out with a Herb Lipchitz.

Herb: You're right. Maybe I should change it.

Me: Good idea.

Herb: How about *Bob* Lipchitz?

Me: Not your first name, moron! Your last name!

Herb: What's wrong with my last name?

Me: Forget it.

Herb: Anyway, to be honest, I miss my ex.

Me: Really? After she plastered pictures of your penis on the internet, you still miss her?

Herb: That wasn't so bad. But let me tell you something. I think she was a Nazi. Did you know she graduated with a double major? Chemical engineering and transportation. Sounds suspicious, don't you think?

Me: She was Jewish!

Herb: Maybe a cover. And there's something else I never told you.

Me: What?

Herb: She was bi-curious.

Me: What does that mean?

Herb: She may have had an interest in women.

Me: How do you know?

Herb: Well, one day she said, "If I don't make love to a woman soon, I'm going to blow my brains out." That's how I knew she was bi-curious.

Me: Sharp thinking, Sherlock.

Herb: But getting back to women, I think I know what the problem is. It's my persona, how I present myself to the public. I'm thinking of changing my image.

Me: To what—Cary Grant?

Herb: Better. Ready? Jay-Z. You know, the rapper who's married to Bounce.

Me: Who?

Herb: Bounce. His wife. I think she's a singer too.

Me: Her name's not Bounce. It's Beyoncé!

Herb: You sure? Looks like Bounce.

Me: I'm sure! So now you're gonna be a rapper?

Herb: That's right. I even got my pickup line. What do you think of this? "Why you always gotta be tripping dogs?" Personally, I don't know why rappers like tripping dogs, but I plan to use it.

Me: It's not "tripping dogs." It's "trippin', dog!" Oh, my God!

Herb: Anyway, I intend to use it. Let's be honest: the women in rap videos look a lot better than those old ladies at Jewish singles events.

Me: Any other gems this evening?

Herb: Yes. There's no such thing as global warming. Case closed.

Me: How'd you come to that conclusion?

Herb: It's just how I feel. Case closed.

Me: Just to let you know—nine out of ten scientists believe in global warming, but if you say "case closed," case closed. Anything else?

Herb: Got a household tip.

Me: Let's hear it.

Herb: Ready? This is amazing. Instead of buying a lint roller, what you can do is wrap packaging tape around your hand and use *that* like a roller! I mean, why spend money on a roller, right?

I stare long and hard at Herb.

Me: What are you getting for dessert?

Herb: Apple pie. How about you?

Me: Vanilla ice cream.

Herb: Vanilla ice cream? Are you crazy? It's cold outside.

Me: What, I'm a reptile—my food depends on outdoor temperature?

Herb: Just saying.

We finish dessert. The waitress brings us the check; we pay and exit the restaurant.

Me: Where you heading?

Herb: PetSmart.

Me: Looking for a wife?

Herb: Ha-ha. No, I need cat food. Same time next week?

Me: I wouldn't miss it for the world.

The following day I call Herb at his place of work.

Me: Get your cat food?

Herb: Yes.

Me: What time did you get home?

Herb: Around midnight.

Me: Why so late?

Herb: On the way back, I saw a sign on the road that said Watch Children, so I sat in the car and waited to see children.

Me: What?

Herb: There was a sign that said Watch Children, so I sat in the car for about two hours, but I didn't see any children. Guess it was past their bedtime, so then I decided to go home.

Me: Oh, my God!

I Was in World War II

My father served in World War II, and he never let me forget it. No matter what difficulty I was going through, his answer was always the same: "I was in World War II!" For example, after my bar mitzvah, I had to write thank-you notes to each guest. At one point I said, "Dad, I've been at it all day. I'm getting tired. I'll finish tomorrow." Without a hint of sympathy, he replied, "You can't write any more bar mitzvah thank-you notes? Well, let me tell you this, young man: I was in World War II!"

No event was too trivial to merit this lesson. If we went out to lunch and I couldn't decide between a chicken salad sandwich and a creamed herring platter, he'd shake his head and say, "So you can't decide between a chicken salad sandwich and a creamed herring platter? Well, let me tell you this, young man: I was in World War II!" So it was whenever I was troubled by a personal setback, spoke in complaint, or was confused about what action to take. Every dilemma elicited the same response: "I was in World War II!"

Despite years of this inevitable pattern, I turned to him for advice when my marriage was crumbling. For I had been told, "Whenever you have a problem, go to your father. He can help you better than anyone." And so I did, although I was nearly certain he'd say little more than "I was in World War II!"

"Dad," I began, "Jen and I are having issues and are seriously considering getting a divorce."

"Have you done everything in your power to save the marriage?" he asked.

"I believe so," I answered, shocked he had not cut me short with "I was in World War II!"

"Have you tried counseling?" he pursued.

"Yes, we've been to a marriage counselor quite a few times," I said, still in a state of disbelief.

"I have a suggestion," he said after a thoughtful pause. "Why don't the two of you go on a vacation? Your mother and I can take care of the kids. I think that would give you time to see if there's any way to preserve your marriage."

"Thank you, Dad. That's a wonderful idea."

"You're welcome, son. But always remember one thing."

"What's that?"

"I was in World War II!"

Toward the end of my father's life, the worn-out line found its purpose. Now in his mid-eighties, beset by crippling diabetes and a myriad of other ailments, he confided, "Son, I don't think I'm gonna make it to another year."

"You mustn't say that," I replied. "Remember what you always told me: 'I was in World War II!' I'm sure, with your determination, you'll make it." And so he did, passing away on January 5, 2008, thus joining the ranks of an illustrious army, all of whom could proudly proclaim, "I was in World War II!"

Dear Target

Dear Target,

May I begin by saying I've been a loyal Target customer for many years. I enjoy so many things about your store: your friendly and helpful staff, the wide variety and excellent selection of products, your competitive prices, and the convenient store hours, to name a few. Of course, I enter Target fully confident you will have whatever I need. However, last Sunday, I could not find my favorite beverage—cherry-flavored club soda. I asked a clerk where it was. He informed me that it was temporarily out of stock, but a new shipment was expected the following day.

Usually, I'm perfectly happy to wait an extra day for a product to arrive. However, on this particular Sunday, I had an uncontrollable craving for cherry-flavored club soda, which led me to conceive the unthinkable—going across the street and buying it at the Acme Market, which I proceeded to do. As soon as I returned home, I drank an entire bottle, which caused me to feel refreshed and invigorated. But then, almost instantly, I was struck by a realization: I had cheated on you no less than a husband cheating on his wife.

Suddenly, pangs of guilt and remorse overwhelmed me. The joy of imbibing the cherry-flavored club soda morphed into feelings of guilt, shame, disgust, and self-loathing. "How could I do this?" I wondered. "How could I cheat on a store that had been so loyal and faithful to me for so many years? Why couldn't I wait one more day to purchase it at Target? How could I have acted so impulsively, like some crazed madman? And further, from what

source did this defect, my lapse into betrayal, spring? From my father? My mother? These torments caused countless sleepless nights.

Therefore, I make the following pledge: I promise never to cheat on you again. Reading the literature on cheating, I realize rebuilding trust takes time and does not come about through mere words. It is achieved through sincere, unflinching action, which I fully intend to perform. I ask only that you find it within yourself to forgive me, though I understand if you cannot, since you are probably as shocked as I am by my unconscionable behavior.

As you may know, we are approaching the Jewish high holidays. Though it is arduous, I am looking forward to Yom Kippur, during which I pray to be inscribed in the Book of Life for another year. But scripture makes clear you cannot ask the Almighty for forgiveness until you have made right any moral transgression against your fellow man or store. Perhaps, then, you can forgive me on or before sunset, September 17 (Yom Kippur), so I can pray to God without the impediment of unfinished business.

Thank you,
Daniel A. Wolf

****

Dear Mr. Wolf,

We at Target were deeply impressed by your letter. Yes, we forgive you and hope you remain a valued customer. May we suggest that the next time you enter Target, you *immediately* visit our pharmacy. May we also remind you that firearms are not permitted anywhere on or near Target premises.

Sincerely,
Target management (as advised by the Department of Homeland Security)

The "Assassination" of Abraham Lincoln

This is the true story of the supposed assassination of Abraham Lincoln. On April 14, 1865, President Lincoln; his wife, Mary Todd Lincoln; Major Henry Rathbone; and the major's fiancée, Clara Harris, attended a performance of *Our American Cousin* at Ford's Theater in Washington, D.C., starring the British-born actress Laura Keene. Lincoln had seen Keene perform a year before and was so appalled by her limited acting skills that he remarked, "If I ever see Keene again, I will blow my brains out." One minute into the play, Lincoln leaned over to Mary and asked who the leading lady was. When she told him it was Laura Keene, he grabbed Major Rathbone's pistol and shot himself.[8]

John Wilkes Booth, an acclaimed actor who was well aware of Lincoln's extraordinary dislike for Keene,[9] attempted to enter the presidential box to prevent the tragedy but was stopped by a guard. A struggle ensued, and by the time Booth entered the box, the terrible deed had been done. He then leaped onto the stage and yelled, *Sic semper tyrannis!* ("Thus always to tyrants!") Historians mistakenly claim this cry was about Lincoln. Instead, it was aimed at Arthur Strasberg,[10] Laura Keene's drama coach, who held tyrannical power over her.

Booth left the theater amid the commotion and met some friends at Mary Surratt's boarding house, where they debated whether theater was dead or just in need of more matinees. Later that evening, Booth was

---

Notes for the Curious

8. Secretary of State William Seward suffered a self-inflicted knife wound that evening. Though not with Lincoln at Ford's Theater, he had accompanied him the year before to see Keene. The memory of that performance so haunted Seward that he attempted to take his own life.

9. Who *wasn't* aware? Lincoln's aversion to Keene was the main topic of conversation throughout the North and some border states from 1864 until the end of the Civil War.

10. Arthur Strasberg was the grandfather of Lee Strasberg, known as "the father of method acting."

informed he was being accused of assassinating Lincoln. He immediately fled and took refuge in a barn, where he remained until Union troops burned him out. His last reported words were "I did not kill the president. I'm just a patsy."

Many books have been written about the death of Abraham Lincoln, but this is the definitive account. Anyone who doesn't accept this story as historically accurate is undoubtedly a conspiracy theorist and most likely wears a tinfoil hat in public—or even in synagogue as a yarmulke.[11]

---

11. Currently, only Reform synagogues allow tinfoil hats as yarmulkes. Though tin is mentioned four times in the Old Testament—Numbers 31:21–23, Ezekiel 22:18, Ezekiel 22:20, and Ezekiel 27:12—there remains heated debate within the Conservative and Orthodox Jewish communities as to whether tinfoil hats can double as yarmulkes.

MISHEGAS¹²

____
12.   Yiddish for craziness

WHO SHALL BE FOR ME

Before Laurel and Hardy, Abbott and Costello, and Martin and Lewis, there was the famous comedy team of Rabbis Hillel and Shammai. They played all the major tents throughout the Middle East during the first century CE. Here they are doing their classic "Who Shall Be for Me," inspired by Hillel's actual line: If I am not for myself, who shall be for me?

Hillel: If I am not for myself, Who shall be for me.

Shammai: Who?

Hillel: That's right.

Shammai: What's right?

Hillel: Who shall be for me.

Shammai: That's what I'm asking.

Hillel: I just told you.

Shammai: Who?

Hillel: Exactly.

Shammai: Who shall be for you?

Hillel: Yes.

Shammai: Yes, what?

Hillel: Who shall be for me.

Shammai: Then who shall be for me?

Hillel: Do you know Who?

Shammai: No.

Hillel: If you don't know Who, don't say Who shall be for me.

Shammai: Who elected you to tell me what I can say?

Hillel: Yes.

Shammai: Yes, what?

Hillel: Who elected me.

Shammai: That's what I'm asking.

Hillel: I just told you.

Shammai: Told me what?

Hillel: Who elected me.

Shammai: Who elected you?

Hillel: Yes. Who knew.

Shammai: Who knew what?

Hillel: Who knew to elect me.

Shammai: Who?

Hillel: Exactly.

Shammai: Who cares?

Hillel: How do you know?

Shammai: How do I know what?

Hillel: How do you know Who cares?

Shammai: I don't know who cares.

Hillel: Then why did you say "Who cares?" if you don't know Who?

Shammai: Can we change the subject?

Hillel: Okay. I'm having a party.

Shammai: Who's coming?

Hillel: Yes.

Shammai: Yes, what?

Hillel: Who's coming.

Shammai: Why you asking me? You should know who's coming.

Hillel: I know Who's coming.

Shammai: Who?

Hillel: I just told you.

Shammai: Told me what?

Hillel: I told you Who's coming.

Shammai: Who?

Hillel: Exactly!

At the Feet (Defeat?) of the Rabbi

Herein are the philosophical musings of Rabbi Moshe ben Yosef Bar Yitzchaki ben Yaakov Shlomo Asher Nachman ben Akiva Mendel Issac Isserles ben Gershom Adin Bezalel ben Meir Alfasi Migash ben Ezra Raphael Geige, known to his friends as Rick. He was born in New York in 1980 and died in 1905. Yes, time not only stood still in the presence of the great teacher but went backward. He was famous for eating with his mouth open, explaining it was essential to keep each orifice open in order to receive the word of God. Unfortunately, this led to a series of arrests for indecent exposure. An avid baseball fan, he is reported to have said, "If I forget thee O Jerusalem may my right hand forget to throw an inside curve at the belt."

On the purpose of life

The purpose of life is to live long. That's it. Live as long as possible because death is the absolute worst thing that could happen. Even when I think about my friends, family, or movies I've seen, I still think death is worse. So just live long.

On wealth

Rabbi Hillel said, "Who is truly rich? He who is content with his portion in life." Yeah, right. Who is truly rich? He who has a lot of stuff. I mean good stuff like electric toothbrushes. He's rich.

On courage

A Chinese philosopher once said, "Wherever man is in danger, I'll be there." He's dead. I'm still living. What good did courage do him?

On sex

Doctors say sex is a natural part of life, like eating and drinking. If that's true, how come I eat and drink more than I have sex?

On friendship

Many women tell me, "We can still be friends." You know what that means. Friendship—it's a joke.

On telephones

Many women tell me, "Don't call me. I'll call you." You know what that means. Telephones—they're a joke.

On foreign affairs

It's good to have an affair with a girl from a foreign country, especially if the girl is from a place where sex is not such a big deal as it is here.

On finding yourself

I found myself a lot, especially in high school.

On scientific development

I support scientific development. I'm especially waiting for the teleport machine, which can instantly transport you to another place. It would come in handy if you're on a miserable date and need to make a quick getaway.

On spiritual symbolism

We can see spiritual symbolism in everyday situations. For example, if a person slips on ice, we should say, "Ah, the spiritual path is truly slippery." If we see someone who appears lost, we should bellow, "Ah, 'tis easy to lose your way while upon the spiritual path." And if we notice a man scratching his butt, we should chime in, "A pilgrim in search of his true self."

On the immediate shut-up

I admire people who can do an immediate shut-up. For example, you're at a party, and everyone's bragging about their golf game. Then Tiger Woods walks in—immediate shut-up. Then everyone's bragging about their travel adventures. Suddenly, Neil Armstrong walks in—immediate shut-up. Finally, everyone's talking about weird rabbis. Then I walk in—immediate shut-up.

On ugliness

Perhaps you know the expression "Everyone has the right to be ugly; just don't abuse the privilege." I wish to go further. With every right, there are responsibilities. Yes, you have the right to be ugly, but you also have the responsibility to stay indoors.

On leadership

Some say great leaders lead from the front. No, great morons lead from the front. I prefer to lead from behind, preferably from some exotic island resort with a 24-hour buffet.

On clash

Newspapers often report "The two sides clashed" when describing a heated debate. Heated as it may be, talking is not clash. When I think clash, I think medieval fighting. Therefore, newspapers ought not to use *clash* unless there's some opportunity for impalement.

On sports

My favorite sport is women's beach volleyball, and if I have to explain why, you're a moron.

On Rosh Hashanah

I prefer the Jewish New Year to the Christian one since I don't need a date nor do I need to spend a fortune on parking.

On the realization you're a schlub

How many games must you lose to realize you're a schlub? For example, you go to a carnival. You try the shooting gallery, throw darts at balloons, or toss rings at floating ducks. Did you go home with the giant bear doll? Of course not, because you're a schlub.

On swimming

I don't understand swimming. It's easier and quicker to walk the length of a pool than swim it. Besides, by walking, you don't get wet. Also, swimmers sometimes swim back to where they started. Why? Did they forget something? And if they forgot something, where can they put it? I don't even want to go there.

On Buddhists and Jews

Buddhists and Jews differ on several key points. While Buddhists seek to hear one's inner voice, Jews seek to know when Early Bird begins. While Buddhists believe desire causes suffering, Jews believe in-laws cause suffering. Finally, while Buddhists do everything in moderation, Jews do everything in excess, especially around a buffet table.

On spelling bees

What's the point of a spelling bee when a computer has spell check? Also, if given a choice between hiring the world's greatest speller or a laptop, I'd choose the latter unless, of course, the world's greatest speller is hot.

On open twenty-four hours

The first time I read a sign saying Open 24 Hours, I thought the store was open for only twenty-four hours before it permanently closed. How strange, I thought, given all the time, energy, and investment just to stay open for twenty-four hours. Someone then explained that Open 24 Hours meant the store stayed open all the time, never closing. He then added, "You're a moron." That was not necessary.

On learning a foreign language

Before deciding to learn a foreign language, I check the girl scene in that country. If women are free with their bodies, I'll study the language and even take an intensive course. However, if women require marriage before sex, I will not learn the language even if there's a promotion.

On forgetting things

We only forget things that are not important to us, like family members. Cynical? No shit, Sherlock!

On poetic justice

Poetic justice is often defined as when something terrible happens to someone who had committed a transgression years before. I have a better definition. It's when lawyers speak in verse. For example, a defense attorney can say:

> My client is innocent
> I truly believe
> Evidence will show
> He ought to be free.

The prosecuting attorney can then say:

> Your honor and jury
> I shall submit
> He's a serial liar
> You must not acquit.

I feel this is a better definition of poetic justice than some crazy story about someone getting their comeuppance years later.

On poetic license

I just paid $300 online for a poetic license. It covers me for five years. People tell me it's a scam, since every writer has poetic license and, therefore, it's not something you pay for. To those, I ask the following: would you trust a dentist if you did not see a diploma? Would you go to a hair salon if you did not notice

a cosmetology license? Would you listen to someone on the radio if they did not possess a Columbia School of Broadcasting certificate? Of course not. Therefore, as a poet, I need to protect myself from frivolous lawsuits.

On philosophy

When reading philosophy, you often see expressions like "One ought to" or "One ought not to." That's fine for one person, but what if there's more than one, like a couple, a trio, or even a foursome? Why doesn't philosophy address those situations?

On reading

People say reading takes you places. No, it doesn't. When I finish reading, I find myself in the same lousy apartment where I first picked up the book.

On mountains

There is a song called "Climb Every Mountain." Who has time for that?

On the dignity of man

In college, I studied the writings of the Italian Renaissance philosopher Pico della Mirandola. His most famous work was *Oration on the Dignity of Man,* in which he wrote: "… because of the divine image planted in him, there are no limits to what man can accomplish" and "Thou shalt have the power out of thy soul's judgment, to be reborn into the higher forms which are divine." Then I get a call from my father to pick him up at Harvey's Bowling Lanes. I go inside, and all I see are fat guys with T-shirts full of tomato sauce and beer stains. Oh yeah, great example of the dignity of man.

On gold

In the song "You're Nobody Till Somebody Loves You" is the line "Gold won't bring you happiness when you're growing old." Really? Try me.

On living in the city vs. living in the suburbs

Recently I've been comparing the advantages of living in the city vs. living in the suburbs. First, the city. You have access to museums, sporting events, concerts, the orchestra, musicals, plays, and ballet. Your friends are nearby, you have a short commute to work, you can walk to a local food market, work out at a local gym, and finally, you have neighbors you can depend on in case of emergency. Next, the advantages of living in the suburbs:

On Big Foot

I've recently completed a personality profile of Big Foot. Here are my findings. First, he's cheap since he never foots the bill. Next, he's socially awkward since he constantly gets off on the wrong foot even if he has a foot in the door. In addition, he's spoiled since Mama Foot waited on him hand and foot. Finally, he hates his father since whenever Big Foot wanted to do something, Papa Foot put his foot down. I hope we find Big Foot soon since he's old and probably has one foot in the grave.

On the Who

I recently attended a Who concert. There are only two Who who are left and both are hard of hearing. Therefore, they should change the name from the Who to the Huh?

On paranoia

We used to say in the 1960s, "Just because you're paranoid doesn't mean no one's watching you," which led to my lifelong love for the double negative.

On Oscar Hammerstein

In the song "You'll Never Walk Alone" Hammerstein wrote, "When you walk through a storm, hold your head up high." Oscar, you were rich. What, you couldn't afford an umbrella?

On haiku poetry

Haiku is a Japanese poem consisting of three lines. The first line has five syllables, the second seven, and the third five. I teach Hebrew Sunday School, and each year I have the children write haiku poetry. Here are some of what the children wrote:

a. I hate my teacher

He is a total douchebag

I can't learn a thing

b. I hate my teacher

I am only eight years old

I can't buy a gun

c. I hate my teacher

He says he is certified

Certified moron

Notice how well the children followed the five-seven-five pattern.

On my mother

I remember when I was growing up, my mother said, "Eat your dinner, or it's going in the trash can." How edifying knowing my dinner was one step away from garbage.

On my brother

My father died twenty years ago, and my brother stole the inheritance. It's okay. I've been getting over it—the last few days.

On stupid things people say

I like to collect stupid things people say. Here's a few:

Princess Diana was alive before she died.

The sun's hot.

It's raining. The roads are wet.

Try not to breathe underwater.

Buying more lottery tickets improves your chances of winning.

He's a salesman. He's trying to sell you something.

On the stupidest thing I ever heard

The stupidest thing I ever heard was "Live each day like it's your last." I figure my last day I'll be hooked up to machines, gasping for air, and getting a sponge bath. Yeah, I think I'll live each day like that.

On dating apps

I started using dating apps. I don't know how they work. Every time I use one, someone delivers a pizza. I've gained twenty pounds using dating apps.

On signs you're getting old

Here are some signs you're getting old: you get a newspaper delivered, you wear a wristwatch, all your parties are in the afternoon, and you pay with cash. That's right, kids, cash!

On transcendental meditation

I practice transcendental meditation. That's an interesting word, transcen-dental. It means "beyond teeth." Since doing transcendental meditation, I have reached new levels of unconsciousness. In fact, just yesterday a truck driver yelled at me, "Hey buddy, you unconscious or somethin'?" How did he know I practice transcendental meditation?

On being a nice guy

I consider myself a nice guy. For instance, I comfort grieving widows, especially those who were left a big house, a couple of cars, and cash. Presently, I'm involved with a widow who goes in and out of consciousness, so I feel it's a good time for financial planning.

On dating suggestions

Young men constantly ask me for dating suggestions. Here's what I tell them:

1. Watch the movie *Titanic*, then go on a dinner cruise.

2. Stuff yourselves at a Chinese buffet, then take a ride on a high-speed rollercoaster.

3. Take part in a baked bean eating competition. Then take her back to your apartment, but keep the windows closed—nothing like humor to break the ice.

On the soundtrack of my life

Here are some excerpts from the soundtrack of my life:

Sorry, we have to cut you. Sure, Harvey's a dwarf, but he shoots better than you.

I wish you could come, but Beverly doesn't like you.

You fit the description. I suggest you get a lawyer.

As your guidance counselor, may I offer two words of advice—aluminum siding.

On history

Many think I'm a historian. Wherever I go, I hear people say, "You're history, pal!"

A Guide for the Confused

In the spirit of *A Guide for the Perplexed*, written in 1190 by the great Jewish philosopher Maimonides, from which we get "Give a man a fish, and you feed him for a day; teach a man to fish, and you feed him for a lifetime," I offer *A Guide for the Confused*. Below are my more salient gems:

If lost, ask someone. If they do not know, you've made a friend for life.

Seek those whose advice makes you horny.

If hungry, eat. If thirsty, drink. If tired, sleep. All else is misery.

Be the giraffe in battle, the hippopotamus in preparation, and the rhinoceros in negotiation. Naturally, this may require a constant change of clothing.

Never assume a person takes on the personality of his or her laundromat.

Simple acts of kindness, strategically placed, can bring tremendous monetary reward. I'm talking gazillions.

Be the orangutan in strategic awareness, the warthog in patient deliberation, and the sloth in battle formation. Again, this may require a constant change of clothing.

Be a friend to naked people.

Act before thinking. It's fun.

Remind your best friend of an embarrassing moment. It's fun.

Reflect upon your life, then pursue with vengeance anyone who gave you advice.

Learn from the past and stay there.

A friend is the consolation prize in your pursuit of a babe or a hunk.

A pet is the consolation prize in your pursuit of a friend.

A wad of cash is more beautiful than a baby's smile.

Speak truth to power lawnmowers.

Judge not a man by his complete lack of intelligence or common sense.

If you did not hear someone's last words, ask him to repeat it.

If you are lost, lonely, aching, and have no home, prepare for bad luck.

Never lie to an electric blanket.

Money is no object unless it follows a verb.

Never trust a word with a silent letter. I swear *whole* is hiding something.

Learn to say no, especially if you stutter on the letter *n*.

Use multiplication to count your blessings. You'll feel better.

Find a woman who is kind, considerate, charitable, wise, supportive, positive, and intelligent. Just don't tell your wife.

Never say death is inevitable unless you can prove it.

Listen to your inner voice, but disregard that which does not conform to subject-verb agreement.

Don't clamp down unless you actually own a set of clamps.

No man is an island. He's either a peninsula, an isthmus, or a strait.

Life is not a popularity contest. It's a beauty contest— and first place you're not.

No need to know from where you came; you're not going that far anyway.

A broken household appliance *is* the end of the world.

You are not the center of the universe; slightly left of center, maybe.

Lost opportunities will come again.

Blame others for your miserable personality. It saves time.

Think not of death as an end but rather as the beginning of a terrible day.

Call no man a coward. He will not hear you as he's running away.

Be humble amongst billionaires.

Listen to losers. They have much to teach you.

Let others plan your life. They can do no worse.

Tell the truth when you're completely alone. Double check to make sure.

The mind is unreliable. Use your sense of touch to know how you feel.

Avoid those who know you.

Imagine how lonely the rich are. I can't either.

You cannot escape your destiny, but try anyway.

Be yourself, though obviously this is not a winning strategy.

Always blend in. Hiding is better.

Your family exists solely as an existential threat.

Have no fixed thoughts. Better, have no thoughts.

Be gracious in defeat.

Eat what's in front of you, not what's behind you.

Remain as ill-defined and nondescript as possible. A political career awaits you.

Don't be fooled by a baby's smile.

Winning is everything, especially against children.

Don't waste time being the best that you can be. You have more important things to do.

Life is short. Dreams take time. Do the math.

Demand respect even though you are wholly undeserving.

Don't respond to insults. There's a better one waiting if you do.

Go to bed early. You've experienced enough torture for one day.

Respond to everything as a personal insult. It will hide the fact that you understand nothing.

Take comfort in knowing there are people worse off than you. It may bring a spring to your step.

Don't bother learning from your mistakes. You're bound to repeat them anyway.

Better to fear the known than the unknown.

Use facial expressions, not words, to convey your thoughts. Admittedly, this may be difficult when using a phone.

A distorted view of life provides great clarity.

Fight to be the last in line.

If you say your pet is your best friend, you might want to work on your social skills.

Give to those less fortunate than you—though it may take time to find such a person.

Never lose sight of the dark.

The world was a beautiful place. Then you came.

Practice perking your ears.

What you lost you never truly had, like your self-respect.

Announce that you know everything—then leave.

Force people to like you.

Rehearse puppy eyes before an important job interview. If necessary, get on all fours and beg.

Seek out sycophants.

Though humor helps create a relaxed working environment, mother jokes don't.

If someone asks why you don't have friends, say they all died in World War II.

Distinguish yourself amongst your friends—wear a crazy hat.

If required to sing for your supper, make sure the song is in the public domain.

Listen to lazy people though it may take all day.

When deciding upon a course of action, don't let trivialities, like your reputation, get in the way.

Think carefully before making a mistake.

If you have a minute to spare, review all you've accomplished in life.

No need to be at a certain place by a certain time. If you didn't go, no-one would notice.

Never trust a sing-along.

Life is short. *Know thyself* takes time. Do the math.

Tread carefully amongst friends.

Lie to yourself. It makes life worth living.

Never contradict a young person. Let life do it.

Never say to a date, "The best things in life are free."

No need to make a new friend. You've experienced enough torture for one day.

Choose your words carefully, then say nothing.

Always admit that you were right.

Never leave a party empty handed.

Practice bragging.

Be the first to arrive at the same conclusion.

Reality is overrated.

Ask new acquaintances highly personal questions. Their reaction is priceless.

Don't be content with idle gossip. Make your gossip come alive!

For heaven's sake—don't bring anyone new into your family.

There's a reason why you have unrecognized talent. Don't make me say it.

Appear essential to every discussion—even if you know nothing about the topic.

When you hear someone say something intelligent or clever, immediately respond with, "You took the words right out of my mouth."

Give in to temptation. You've already given in to everything else.

Go where no man would even think of going.

Challenge yourself to a duel.

Be generous with your time. Give people clocks.

Never hesitate to say, "I need a few days to think about that."

Sleep with confidence.

EIGHTY QUESTIONS TO PONDER

In light of the Jewish tradition to question every little thing, I submit eighty questions to ponder:

1. If man were endowed with a booming voice, would we still need telephones?

2. Do birds say, "So-and-so has left the building"?

3. Would humans exist if the first man had been shy?

4. Should people be forced to reminisce?

5. Should people who tire of wearing latex suits at sex clubs cut them into gloves, swimming caps, and party balloons before donating to Goodwill?

6. What were Mister Ed's last words?

7. If Jesus had worn braces, would he have said, "Dentist, Novocaine thyself!"?

8. If a bullet bounced off Superman and killed a bystander, would Superman be an accomplice to murder?

9. If pigs could suddenly fly, would that compel people to do things they said they'd never do?

10. Since the *m-a-n* in Berman is pronounced *min*, should Batman be pronounced *Batmin*?

11. If laughter is the best medicine, can comedians apply for a medical license?

12. Do Robert's Rules of Order apply in a sauna?

13. Does the killing of an obese person constitute mass murder or at least multiple homicide?

14. If dogs could talk, would they ever shut up?

15. Since King Kong climbed the Empire State Building instead of taking the elevator, should his handlers be required to pay the elevator fee?

16. How vital is mood in suspense drama?

17. Can a double amputee enter a nudist colony even though he's half-naked?

18. Should the Transylvania Police Department be reprimanded for not having an officer stationed at the blood bank in their pursuit of Dracula?

19. Who was more attractive—Marilyn Monroe or the fifth president of the United States, James Monroe?

20. Who had a more significant impact on events leading up to and including the American Civil War—Abraham Lincoln or jazz vocalist Abbie Lincoln (1930-2010)?

21. If you're caught robbing a food bank, could you be charged with bank robbery?

22. Should torturers be good at algebra?

23. Who was stronger—Napoleon Bonaparte or my dog, who could tear a bone apart?

24. When a Frenchman steps in doo-doo, does it go "squish" or "quiche"?

25. If you were a hostess at Olive Garden, would you seat Donner, party of five?

26. Do cannibals ever go on a diet? If so, what body parts do they give up?

27. Exactly how annoying was Frederick Douglass?

28. What did Jesus serve those who were allergic to fish? And could they get seconds?

29. Did Vincent van Gogh believe everything he heard?

30. Should stealing the covers be classified as a felony?

31. Do cyclops leer?

32. Why speak to an ex-pert when you can speak to an actual working pert?

33. Can spilling Mountain Dew on someone be classified as "Do unto others"?

34. Should the last remaining rock promoter say, "Except for the thermonuclear war, how was the show?"

35. Does it really matter if the tallest man on earth combs his hair?

36. Since the Bible mentions only breakfast and dinner (Exodus 16:12), should eating lunch be punishable by stoning?

37. In light of the pandemic, should the Phantom of the Opera double-mask it?

38. Would Horace Greeley have said, "Go West, young man," if he had lived in California?

39. Did Jack the Ripper commit suicide because he felt the name "Jack the Ripper" might unduly influence a jury?

40. Should the ability to whistle a happy tune affect a jury's decision?

41. Who gave the go-ahead to use the term "Go ahead"?

42. Which led to the decline of the Wild West—the introduction of the criminal justice system or dentistry?

43. If Einstein were alive during hip-hop, would he have formulated E=MC Hammer?

44. Did Abraham Lincoln sign the Emancipation Proclamation during a game of Truth or Dare?

45. How drunk was Frank Sinatra when he allowed Joey Bishop to join the Rat Pack?

46. As a child, did Jeffrey Dahmer play with his classmates or eat them?

47. Is a beautiful, warm, spring like day overrated?

48. Exactly how annoying was Susan B. Anthony?

49. Did Elvis Presley really dance, or was he just high-strung?

50. Did the Kennedy brothers go into politics because they couldn't doo-wop?

51. If children are the future, why are they here now?

52. As a child, did Donald Trump build sandcastles or hotels?

53. How many years did Dr. Jonas Salk waste telling people it was the *Salk* vaccine and not the *Salt* vaccine?

54. Should police be called to a pillow fight?

55. Was the Birdman of Alcatraz eligible for frequent-flyer miles?

56. When Jackie Kennedy confronted her husband about his infidelities, did he respond by saying, "Ask not"?

57. How difficult was it for Robert James, father of bank robbers Frank and Jesse James, to decide which one was the black sheep of the family?

58. Was there ever a better listener than Al Capone's cellmate?

59. Did Attila the Hun refer to himself as Attila the Hun to distinguish himself from those simply named Attila?

60. Can a bald person experience a hair-raising event?

61. Do male penguins tell marriage counselors, "My wife is frigid"?

62. When pigs make love, do they say, "Talk clean to me"?

63. Since open mic sets are five minutes or less, should comedians skip the set-up and go directly to the punch line?

64. Is it politically correct for a person of color to tell an off-color joke?

65. Do breads joke, "You're toast"?

66. If a cavewoman wife wanted to kill her caveman husband, did she serve him cooked food?

67. Do male turtles ask female turtles, "How 'bout a slowy?"

68. Do cannibals joke, "Hi, Hamburger—I mean Harvey"?

69. If money can't buy happiness, how else can you buy happiness?

70. If someone carries a 12-inch ruler at all times, does that person have a foot fetish?

71. Do depressed porcupines say, "What's the point?"

72. Since the dawn of creation was there ever a luckier man than Ringo Starr?

73. If a person claims to possess the third eye of spiritual enlightment but makes poor life decisions, should he or she visit an optometrist?

74. Did General Lee get confused whenever he heard the word *generally*?

75. How did the judge react when the Boston Strangler said before sentencing, "Hey, judge—can you cut me some slack?"

76. Since smiling is contagious, when will a vaccine be available?

77. Do adult cats look at kitty porn?

78. How cruel is it for a robber to say, "You got ten seconds to hand it over" if the victim can't tell time?

79. Did Hercules belong to a gym? If so, what type of membership did he have?

80. Who put the fun in erectile dys*fun*ction?

QUIT

In response to the poem "Don't Quit" by John Greenleaf Whittier, as featured in the above story "Sound Advice," I have penned a persuasive rebuttal, "Quit."

> When signs say All Are Welcome
> But you they don't admit
> One thing left for you to do
> Quit
>
> With everything you tell your kids
> They call you hypocrite
> One thing left for you to do
> Quit
>
> The Elephant Man is on the team
> But you they call unfit
> One thing left for you to do
> Quit
>
> When you open up the paper
> And you're in the obit
> One thing left for you to do
> Quit
>
> When trading jokes with a child

And he displays more wit
One thing left for you to do
Quit

Your mother's stock is at new highs
But your stock takes a hit
One thing left for you to do
Quit

When your friends give you a present
It's a suicide kit
One thing left for you to do
Quit

When you receive your salary
The money's counterfeit
One thing left for you to do
Quit

When you meet the Dalai Lama
And cause a raging fit
One thing left for you to do
Quit

The Magic Trick

Henry and Phil meet by chance inside a mall.

Phil: Henry!

Henry: Phil, nice to see you again. Doin' some shopping?

Phil: Not really. Just escaping from the heat outside.

Henry: I can understand that. Why shvitz[13] when you can come into a nice air-conditioned place?

Phil: That's right. So how's everything over there?

Henry: Over where?

Phil: Over there, where you're standing.

Henry: But I'm right here.

Phil: Yes, from your perspective, you're here. But from my perspective, you're over there.

Henry: Listen, I'm no grammarian, but it seems you say "over there" when there's some distance between things.

Phil: How much distance?

---

13.   **Shvitz:** Sweat.

Henry: I don't know. Maybe a few feet, but more than a few inches. Can we move on? Anything new in your life?

Phil: Glad you asked. I've been studying magic.

Henry: Really? Can you show me something?

Phil: Sure. Let me do my favorite trick. I'm going to disappear.

Henry: This I've got to see . . . or not see—ha, ha, ha.

Phil: Let's begin. Where am I?

Henry: You're in front of me.

Phil: Right. I'm standing directly in front of you. Now I want you to close your eyes and count to three. Then open your eyes. Ready?

Henry: Ready.

Phil: Begin.

Henry closes his eyes and begins to count.

Henry: One . . . two . . .

Phil moves to Henry's side.

three!

Henry opens his eyes.

Phil: There—I disappeared.

Henry: No, you didn't. You just moved.

Phil: Am I in front of you?

Henry: No.

Phil: So I disappeared.

Henry: You did not disappear! You just moved from over there . . .

Henry points to where Phil was previously standing.

            to here.

Phil: I moved from where?

Henry: *(points again)* Over there.

Phil: Aha! You said, "Over there." Get it?

Henry: You're nuts. I have to go.

Henry attempts to leave.

Phil: Come on, Henry, I'm only playing with ya.

Henry stops, turns to face Phil.

Henry: Forget it. Talking to you's hard.

Phil: What's hard?

Henry: Talking to you.

Phil: Talking's not hard. Look! I put my hand near my mouth.

Phil puts his hand near his mouth.

            Now I speak. What comes out?

Henry: Air.

Phil: Is air hard?

Henry: You're insane.

Phil: Is air hard? Answer the question.

Henry: Air is not hard.

Phil: So how can talking be hard?

Henry: Phil, do the world a favor—drop dead.

Phil: I can do that. Close your eyes. Count to three . . .

ANIMALS WITH ATTITUDES

TWO JEWISH ELEPHANTS

Two Jewish elephants happen to meet in the middle of a field.

Rose: Your baby's so cute. Shayna punim![14] Mazel tov![15]

Heddi: Thank you.

Rose: I love the way he walks with that little wiggle. You could plotz.[16] And the way he drags his trunk. He must be an absolute joy.

Heddi: He is. That's why I prefer you stay away from him.

Rose: What?

Heddi: You heard me. Stay away from him if you know what's good for you.

Rose: Why you acting like this? I'm saying how lucky you are to have such a lovely son. What's with the attitude?

---

14.   **Shayna punim:** Beautiful face.
15.   **Mazel tov:** Good luck.
16.   **Plotz:** Explode.

Heddi: What's with the attitude? I'll tell you what's with the attitude. I've heard what you tell others about him—how he's such a klutz, and blah blah blah. So now you're trying to schmooze?[17] That don't wash with me, girlfriend. Just stay away from him.

Rose: Wait a minute. You have the whole thing backward. I never once said anything bad.

Heddi: That's not what I heard.

Rose: Well, you heard wrong.

Heddi: Did I? You've been jealous from the day I had him. Everyone's kvelling,[18] swinging their trunks—everyone, that is, except you. Think I didn't notice? Whispering to Mae I was too old to be a mother, and what you said to Sylvia I won't even go there. And excuse me, but what kind of baby shower present was that?

Rose: You didn't like it?

Heddi: Like it? It was a tchotchke,[19] for God's sakes. Where did you get that, some dollar store? So I never wanna speak to you again. If we happen to pass each other at a watering hole, make like I'm not there.

Rose: You can't even trumpet?

Heddi: Maybe someday, but not now. Better we should go our separate ways. I think that's for the best.

Rose: For you but not for me. Come on. We've known each other since we were calves. We used to play under our mothers' tucheses.[20] Doesn't that mean anything to you?

Heddi: Sure it does. I'm human, aren't I?

Rose: Uh, no, you're not.

---

17.   **Schmooze:** Chat, make small talk.
18.   **Kvell:** Experience pride in someone.
19.   **Tchotchke:** Trinket, little toy.
20.   **Tuches:** Butt, behind.

Heddi: *(pause)* Right. Let me go. It's time for his nap.

Rose: I'm so vermischt.[21]

Heddi: Well, you should have thought about that before you said those things.

Heddi exits. Rose remains, dejected, trunk dragging on ground.

____

21.   **Vermischt:** Confused, mixed up.

Two Jewish Lions

Two Jewish lions, Gary and Bill, are sleeping as morning breaks. Bill wakes up, stretches, looks around, and starts walking away. Gary wakes up.

Gary: Where you going?

Bill: I'm hungry. I'm gonna hunt for food.

Gary: I'm hungry too. Let's go together. Two's better than one. Then we can strategize.

Bill: That's okay. I'm sure I can catch something alone.

Gary: Don't be meshuggah.[22] We've always hunted together. Now you want to go alone? It makes no sense. Is there a problem?

Bill: Not at all. I feel like hunting alone.

Gary: No, something's the matter. I can sense it. Come on, tell me. It's something I said last night, right?

Bill: No. You were in fine form.

Gary: Then what's bothering you?

Bill: All right, it's something you said.

---

22.   **Meshuggah:** Crazy, insane.

Gary: I thought so. Well, if I offended you, I'm sorry. You know I was only kidding. I would never say anything to hurt you.

Bill: I'm not referring to that. No, it's something else.

Gary: You mean . . . ?

Bill: That's right.

Gary: I thought you liked I'm always honest.

Bill: Not *that* honest. Did you seriously believe I could accept such a thing?

Gary: Frankly speaking, yes. I thought you could.

Bill: Well, I can't. My God, how can you live with that? Such a thing—a shanda![23] Feh![24]

Gary: I just thought . . .

Bill: Thought what—I could let it pass? Say, "Well, that's the way he is. All lions are different"? Didn't you notice how everyone got so quiet? Not a single roar. Fred was ready to call the authorities till I talked him out of it. And you can forget about the lionesses. I admit the males are nothing to look at with all their drooling, but what female could go with you without falling a few notches in the hierarchy? Which brings me to my next point: I'm not sure how we can remain friends. Everyone will become suspicious if they see us together. I'm not proud of myself for saying this. Friendship is something I've always placed a high premium on, but I have a reputation to uphold, and I can't be seen with someone of such extreme moral turpitude.

Gary looks down.
          Look at me!
Gary looks up.

---

23.   **Shanda:** A scandal.
24.   **Feh:** Expression of disgust.

You're a good cat. Get some help, and maybe we can get together. After all, I like to kibitz. Who else can do it? Fred? Forget it. Okay?

Gary: What did I say? A bissel.[25]

Bill: You call that a bissel? Come on, that was no bissel. I have to go. Don't worry. You'll be fine.

Bill exits.

Gary: Oy vey iz mir.[26]

____

25.   **Bissel:** A little bit.
26.   **Oy vey iz mir:** Woe is me.

Two Jewish Housecats

Two Jewish housecats, Sid and Duke, meet in the living room. Sid is Duke's senior by a few cat years.

Duke: Can you believe it? The owner got a dog! He's already chased me around the basement. What should we do?

Sid: What do you mean, "we"?

Duke: "We" means *we*. Us. Both. He'll come after you, too, shortly.

Sid: Don't call me "Shortly."

Duke: This is no time for jokes. We need a plan.

Sid: What plan? We don't need a plan.

Duke: Are you serious? We're not talking dumb puppy here. He's dangerous.

Sid: Dangerous, shmangerous. We're cats, remember? We know how to scurry. Or did you forget how to scurry?

Duke: I know how to scurry. I just think we need some early-warning system—you know, inform each other if one of us sees him coming.

Sid: You've been sitting on too many TVs. What early-warning system? He comes after you, you run. He comes after me, I run. There—that's the plan.

Duke: You don't seem to appreciate the urgency of the situation. This is no ordinary dog. He's big, fast, and committed. Sid, come on. Don't you care what happens to us?

Sid: To *us*? I think you mean to *you*. And my answer is quite simple—I don't care what happens to you. You've been a noodge[27] for years, kvetching[28] about every little thing: "There's not enough milk." "I can't find my blanket." "Where's the owner? He should have been home by now." What, the whole house has to revolve around you? And another thing—can't you read a face? Do I look interested in what you have to say? Fortunately, cats can feign sleep, so that's what I do when you start your mishegas.[29] Then, as soon as you leave, I scamper about. Do I worry that the owner bought a dog? Of course. It will make life much more difficult. On the other hand, I see it as an opportunity, 'cause maybe that hound will put an end to you, and I can live out my September years in some peace.

Duke: I don't know what to say. I never knew you felt like this.

Sid: Well, if you could stop munching your balls for five seconds, you might notice how I feel. You must be the lamest-brained cat on the planet. Doesn't it ever cross your mind to do some mischief—like knock over a flowering plant, chew some paper plates, grab a fish from the fishbowl?

Duke: No.

Sid: Why not?

Duke: The owner wouldn't like it. And besides, I like fish. They're cute.

Sid: I'm having a stroke. Who the hell cares what the owner likes? Your name's Duke—so live up to it. Don't I live up to my name—Sid—like some smart ass?

Duke: But the owner calls you "Sidney," not "Sid."

-----

27.   **Noodge:** Pest, whiner.
28.   **Kvetch:** Complain.
29.   **Mishegas:** Craziness.

Sid: Say that name again, and I'll claw your eyes out. "Oh, Sidney, where are you, Sidney?" I get this namby-pamby name, and they call you "Duke." You're as Duke as a three-legged table. Where's the justice in that?

Duke: Calm down. It's only a name. It's not important.

Sid: It is to me.

Duke: *(pause, then relentlessly)* Have you thought about a plan?

Sid: *(pause, then wearily)* If you're noshing[30] and I see him coming, I'll tell you, and you do the same for me.

Duke: That's the spirit!

Duke appears triumphant while Sid's face conveys resignation.

---

30.   **Nosh:** Eat.

Two Jewish Rhinoceroses

(or Rhinoceri for those who like to nitpick)

Jack and Marvin meet on an open field in the African savanna.

Jack: Marvin, why so down in the dumps?

Marvin: You'd be down too if your head weighed a ton.

Jack: You got a point.

Marvin: But you're right. I *am* in the dumps.

Jack: What happened?

Marvin: *(takes a deep breath)* I'm getting married.

Jack: You're getting married? That's great! Who's the lucky cow?

Marvin: Hey, watch it! That's not nice.

Jack: A "cow" is a female rhino. Don't you know that?

Marvin: Sorry, I forgot.

Jack: Never mind. How did you meet?

MARVIN

Marvin: We were both rolling in mud and bumped into each other. It was love at first bump, you could say.

Jack: That's wonderful. What's her name?

Marvin: Gulika.

Jack: Gulika? What kind of name is Gulika?

Marvin: It means *pearl* in Hindi.

Jack: What's Hindi?

Marvin: It's the official language of India.

Jack: What are you talking about, "India"?

Marvin: She's an Indian rhino.

Jack: An *Indian* rhino?

Marvin: That's right.

Jack: How did she wind up in Africa?

Marvin: Beats me. A faulty sense of direction, I guess.

Jack: What's her last name?

Marvin: Kapoor.

Jack: Ka *what?*

Marvin: Kapoor.

Jack: Kapoor? Doesn't sound Jewish to me.

Marvin: It's not. She's Hindu.

Jack: What's Hindu?

Marvin: Nothing. What's hin with you? Little joke, ha-ha.

Jack: A comedian you're not. So tell me, what's Hindu?

Marvin: It's the main religion of India.

Jack: So you're going to convert?

Marvin: No. I'm Jewish, and I intend to stay Jewish. Don't I look Jewish?

Jack: Absolutely.

Marvin: Right? *(getting excited)* I mean, look at my two beautiful horns. I know they say Jewish rhinos have big horns, but I don't care. I love my horns. I'm proud of my horns. I can't imagine life without my horns. I wake up every day admiring my *two* beautiful, magnificent, splendiferous horns!

Jack: Marvin, why you getting so excited about your horns?

Marvin: Because Gulika is an Indian rhino.

Jack: I know. You told me.

Marvin: Don't you see the problem? Can't you put two and two together and guess why I'm so depressed?

Jack: No.

Marvin: For God's sakes, Jack, Indian rhinos have only one horn, and she demands I get a horn job so we look the same.

Jack: A horn job?

Marvin: That's right. She wants me to have one horn removed.

Jack: You mean a rhinoplasty?

Marvin: A what?

Jack: A rhinoplasty. It's a medical procedure to remove a horn.

Marvin: A medical procedure named after *us*? Kinda makes ya feel proud.

Jack: Are you going to do it?

Marvin: I'm thinking about it.

Jack: Thinking about it? Are you crazy? You'll look ridiculous walking around with one horn. Of course, no one will say anything to your face, but believe me, you'll be the topic of conversation throughout the entire savanna. I know the lodge will kick you out, and you can forget about our weekly card game.

Marvin: But I love her!

Jack: Love, shmove. You can't do a thing like that. You tell her, "Take me as I am, all 4,000 pounds— or we're history."

Marvin: But it's my last chance to find true love.

Jack: You call that love? Mutilating yourself? What, circumcision wasn't enough? Now you have to cut a horn too? Forget it. That's not love. That's control. You give in on a thing like that, and you can kiss any freedom goodbye. That's it. Lie down in mud and tell her how you feel. If she still insists, roll yourself up and walk away.

Marvin: Thanks, Jack. I needed that.

Jack: Look! I see a crash of rhinos. Why don't we crash the crash?

Marvin: That joke never gets old. Let's go, buddy.

ABOUT THE AUTHOR

Daniel Wolf was born and raised in Philadelphia, Pennsylvania. He retired from the Philadelphia Public School system in June 2015, having taught English as a Second Language for twenty-four years, primarily at the elementary level. In addition, from 1983 to 1993, he lived and taught English in Japan, during which time he traveled extensively both in Japan and throughout Asia.

In addition to being a short-story writer, Mr. Wolf has composed five complete musicals (book, music, and lyrics) and has published five plays, all of which can be viewed at www.danielwolfmusic.com

He also performs stand-up comedy throughout the Philadelphia region. You can view his comedy routines and music videos on his YouTube channel: *Daniel Wolf music & comedy*. Other interests include chess, traditional Japanese archery (kyudo), cycling, nature walks, and exotic cuisine. He can be reached at wolfdnl@comcast.net

The End

We are all the same on the inside.

I am biracial, and that's okay!!

Skin color and race does not matter.

is love and what is on the inside.

She urged to embrace what God has given me because what matters the most

I was Created perfectly by God
and I am more than enough!

Mommy said that my skin color
or my hair texture does not matter.

I get to experience two different races,
cultures, backgrounds, and religions.

Mommy said that I have
the best of both worlds.

right in the middle.

I am somewhere

Or that my hair is not straight enough.

Then with Daddy's family,
I do not feel like I am light enough.

When I am with Mommy's family,
I sometimes feel like I am not dark enough.
Or that my hair is not curly enough.

Daddy is Puerto Rican, and his skin is tan like the color of sand at the beach.

This makes me biracial with skin the color of caramel.

Mommy is African American, and her skin is brown like the color of honey.

Some families have different skin colors.
I come from a very different family.
Being different is okay!

Some families have the same skin color.

Families can be quite different.

For Savannah

Illustrator: Kat Powell

Publisher: Bruised and Unbroken
ISBN: 978-1-7350368-2-3

I Am Biracial and That's Okay

By: Dr. Shareeda Tyaire